Dear Parent:

Psst . . . you're looking at the Super Secret Weapon of Reading. It's called comics.

STEP INTO READING® COMIC READERS are a perfect step in learning to read. They provide visual cues to the meaning of words and helpfully break out short pieces of dialogue into speech balloons.

Here are some terms commonly associated with comics:

PANEL: A section of a comic with a box drawn around it.
CAPTION: Narration that helps set the scene.
SPEECH BALLOON: A bubble containing dialogue.
GUTTER: The space between panels.

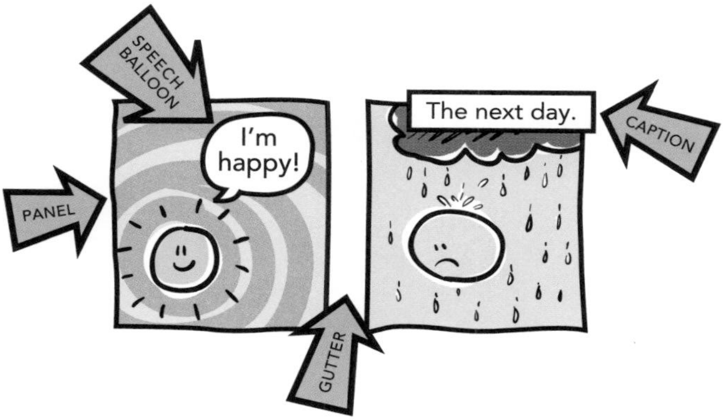
SPEECH BALLOON
I'm happy!
PANEL
The next day.
CAPTION
GUTTER

Tips for reading comics with your child:

- **Have your child read the speech balloons while you read the captions.**
- **Ask your child: What is a character feeling? How can you tell?**
- **Have your child draw a comic showing what happens after the book is finished.**

STEP INTO READING® COMIC READERS are designed to engage and to provide an empowering reading experience. They are also fun. The best-kept secret of comics is that they create lifelong readers. ***And that will make you the real hero of the story!***

Jennifer L. Holm and Matthew Holm
Co-creators of the Babymouse and Squish series

© 2023 Sesame Workshop. Sesame Street Mecha Builders™ and associated characters, trademarks, and design elements are owned and licensed by Sesame Workshop. All rights reserved. Published in the United States by Random House Children's Books, a division of Penguin Random House LLC, 1745 Broadway, New York, NY 10019, and in Canada by Penguin Random House Canada Limited, Toronto, in conjunction with Sesame Workshop.

Step into Reading, Random House, and the Random House colophon are registered trademarks of Penguin Random House LLC.

Visit us on the Web!
www.sesamestreet.org
rhcbooks.com

Educators and librarians, for a variety of teaching tools, visit us at RHTeachersLibrarians.com

ISBN 978-0-593-64459-1 (trade) — ISBN 978-0-593-64461-4 (ebook) —
ISBN 978-0-593-64460-7 (lib. bdg.)

Printed in the United States of America
10 9 8 7 6 5 4 3 2 1

Random House Children's Books supports the First Amendment and celebrates the right to read.

A COMIC READER

STEP INTO READING®

STEP 2

SESAME STREET

MECHA BUILDERS™

Roll, Chickens, Roll!

adapted by Lauren Clauss
based on the episode "Roll, Chickens, Roll!"
written by Scott Gray
illustrated by Shane Clester

Random House New York

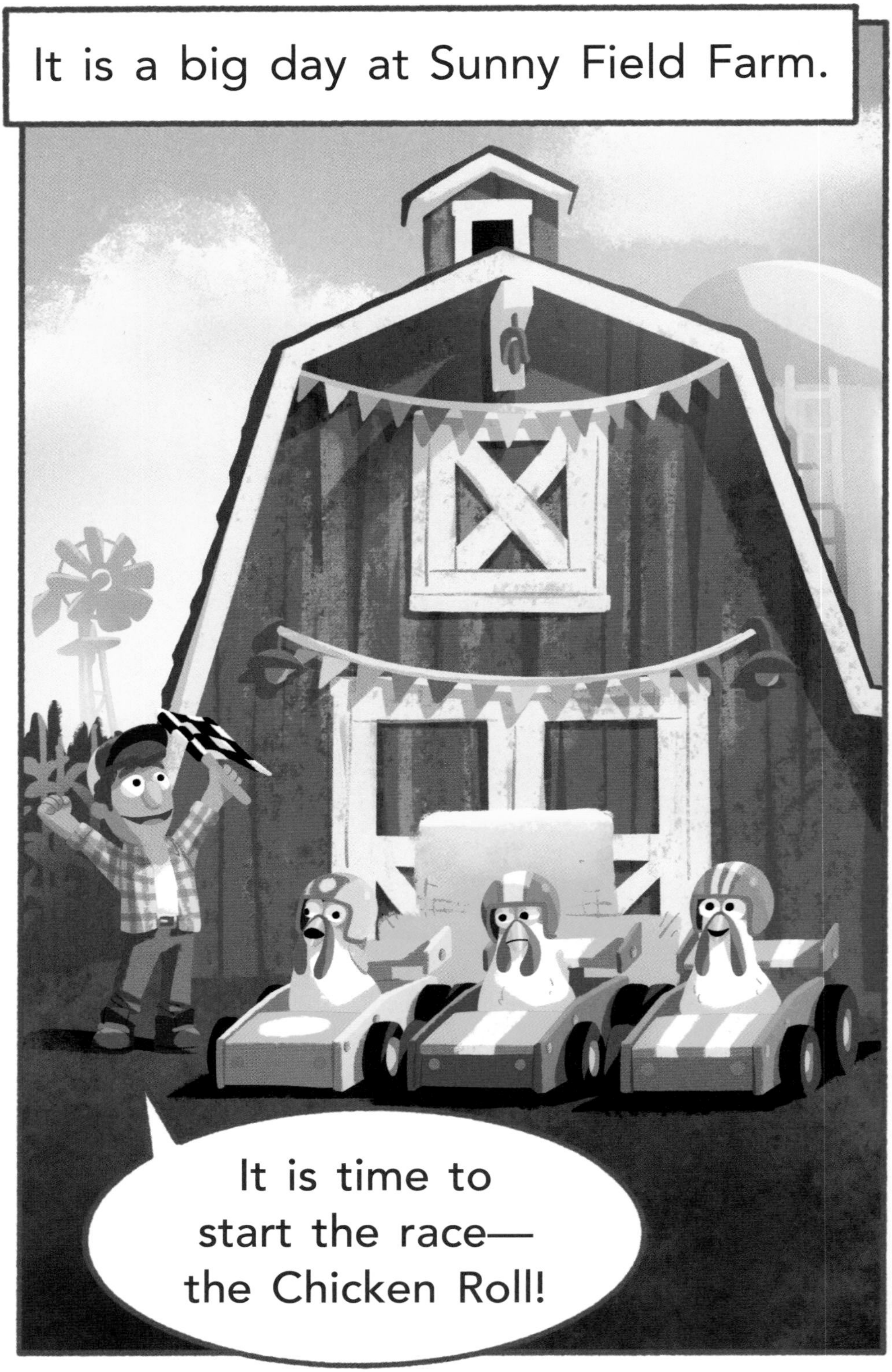
It is a big day at Sunny Field Farm.
It is time to start the race— the Chicken Roll!

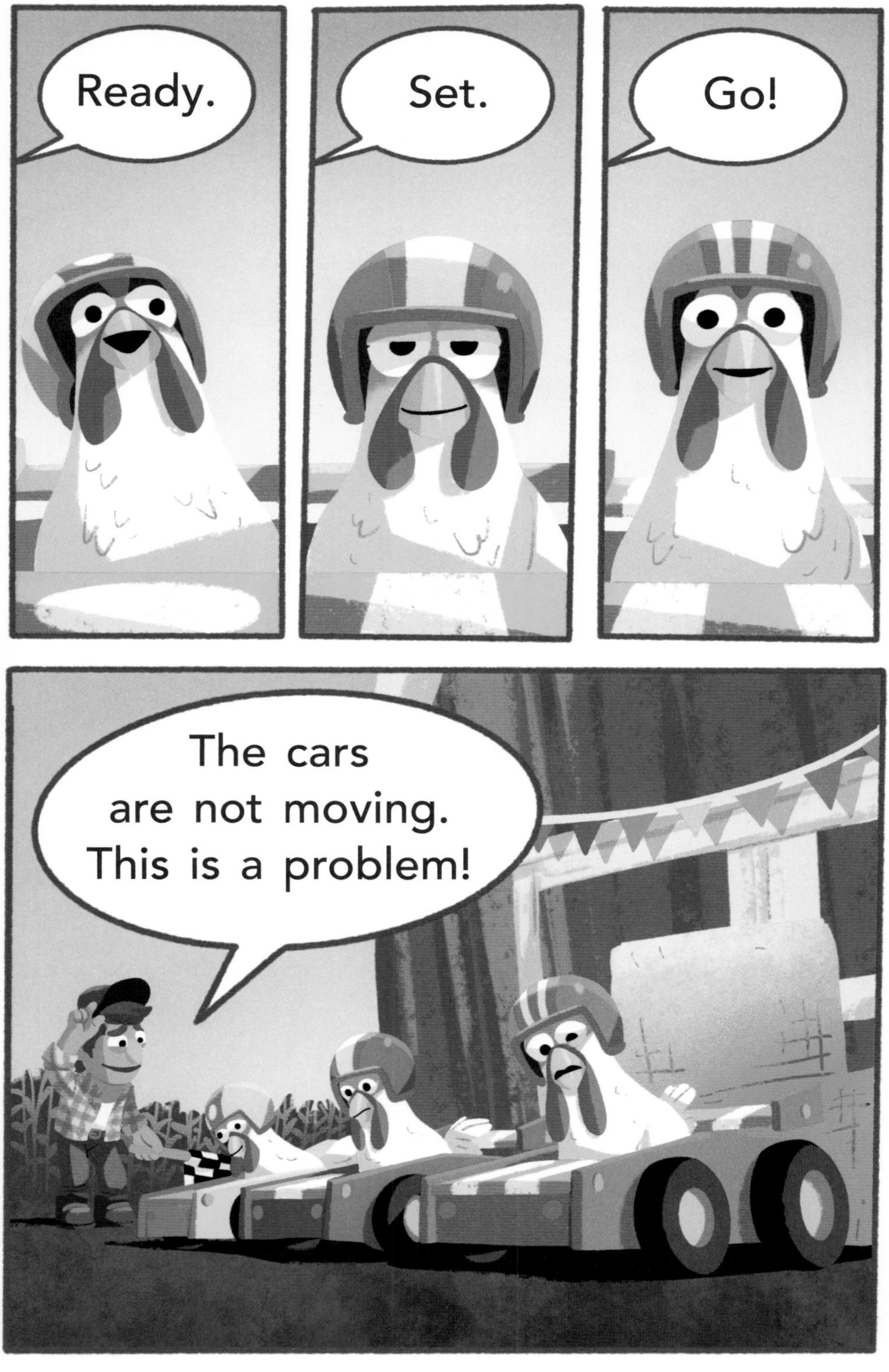
Ready.
Set.
Go!
The cars are not moving. This is a problem!

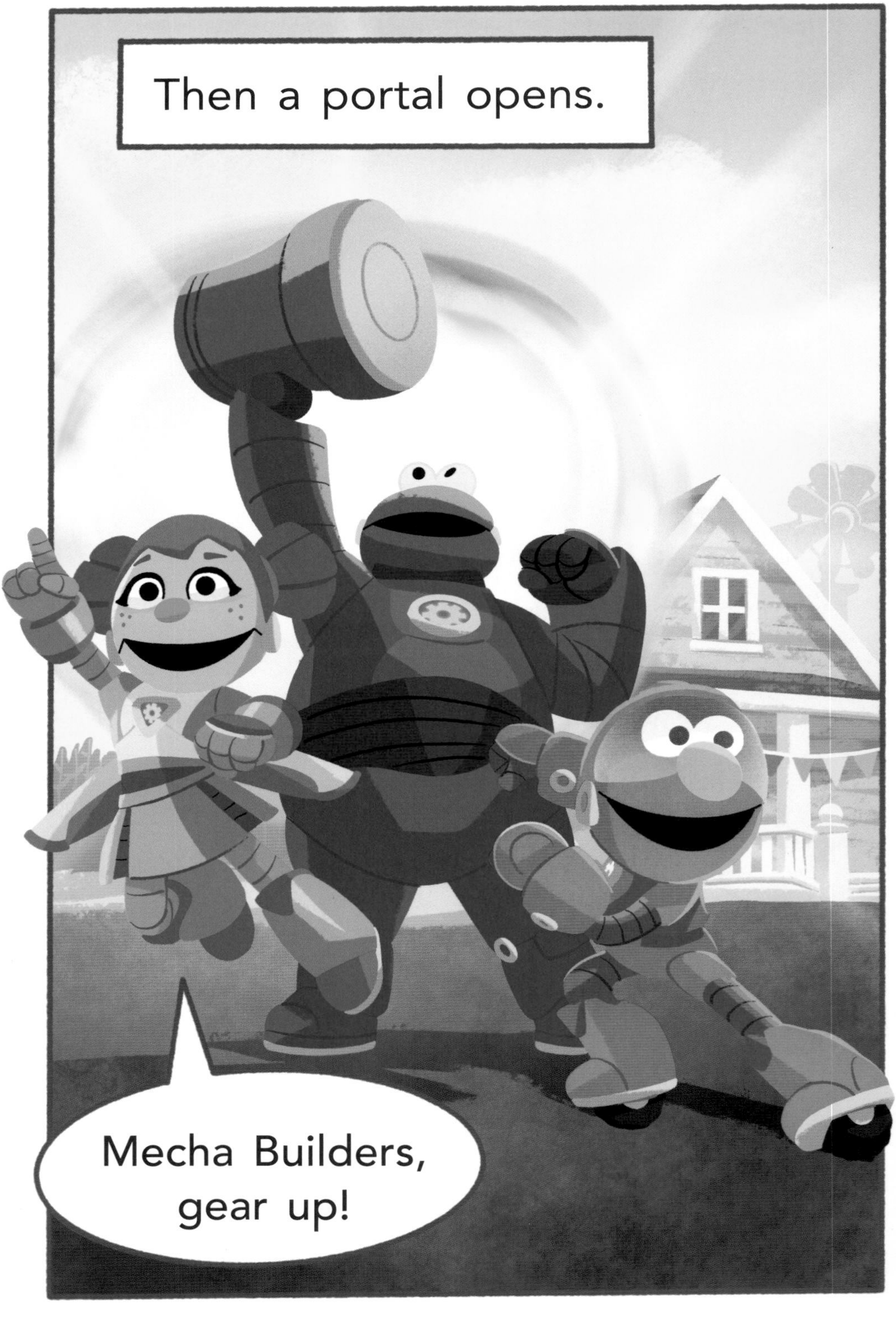
Then a portal opens.
Mecha Builders, gear up!

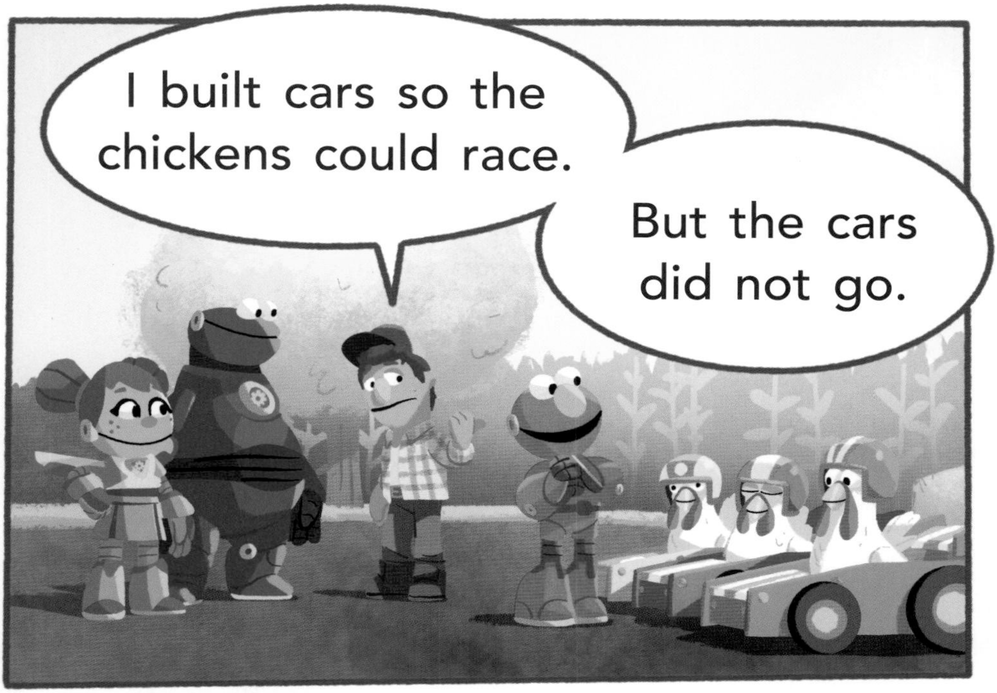
I built cars so the chickens could race.
But the cars did not go.

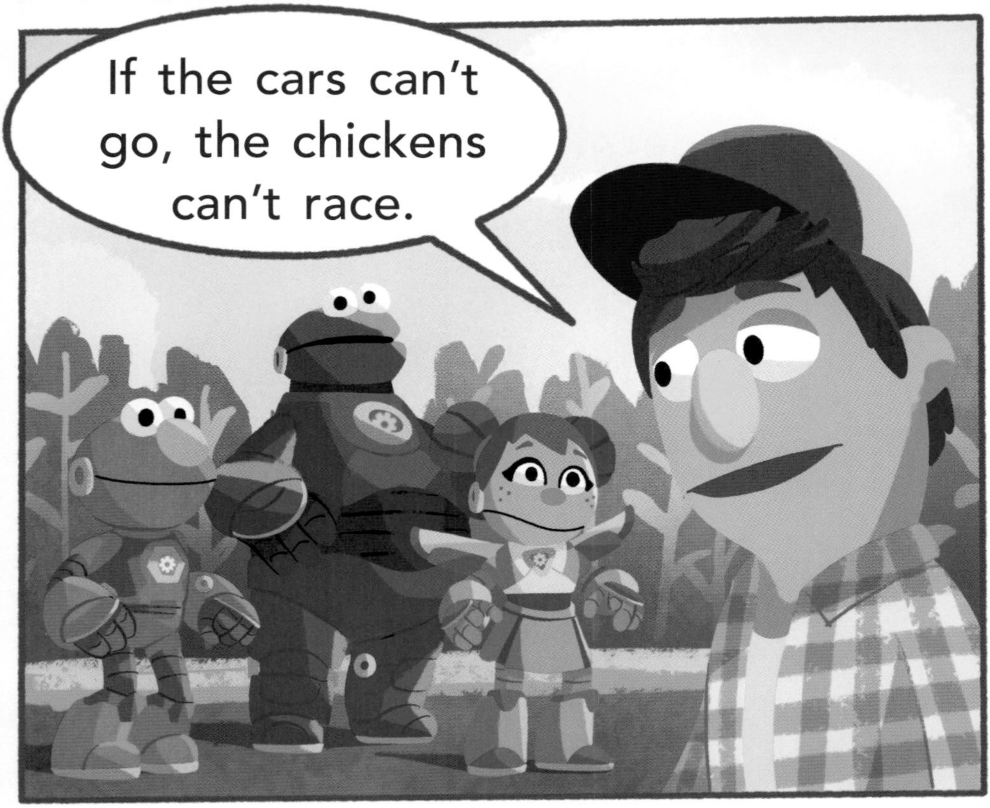
If the cars can't go, the chickens can't race.

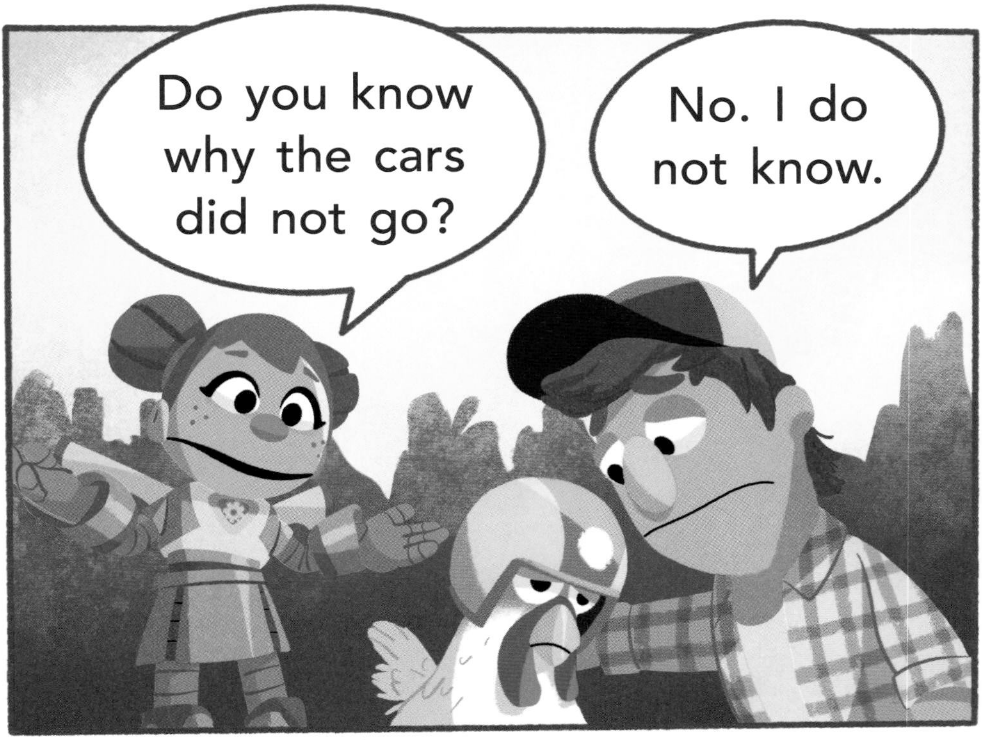
Do you know why the cars did not go?
No. I do not know.

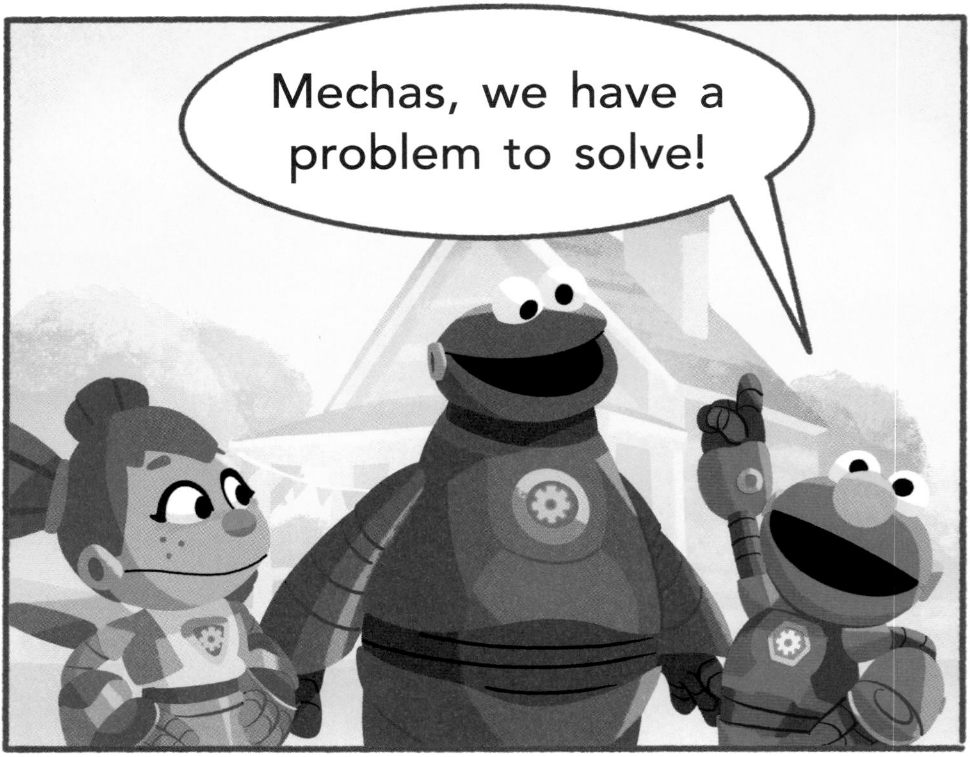
Mechas, we have a problem to solve!

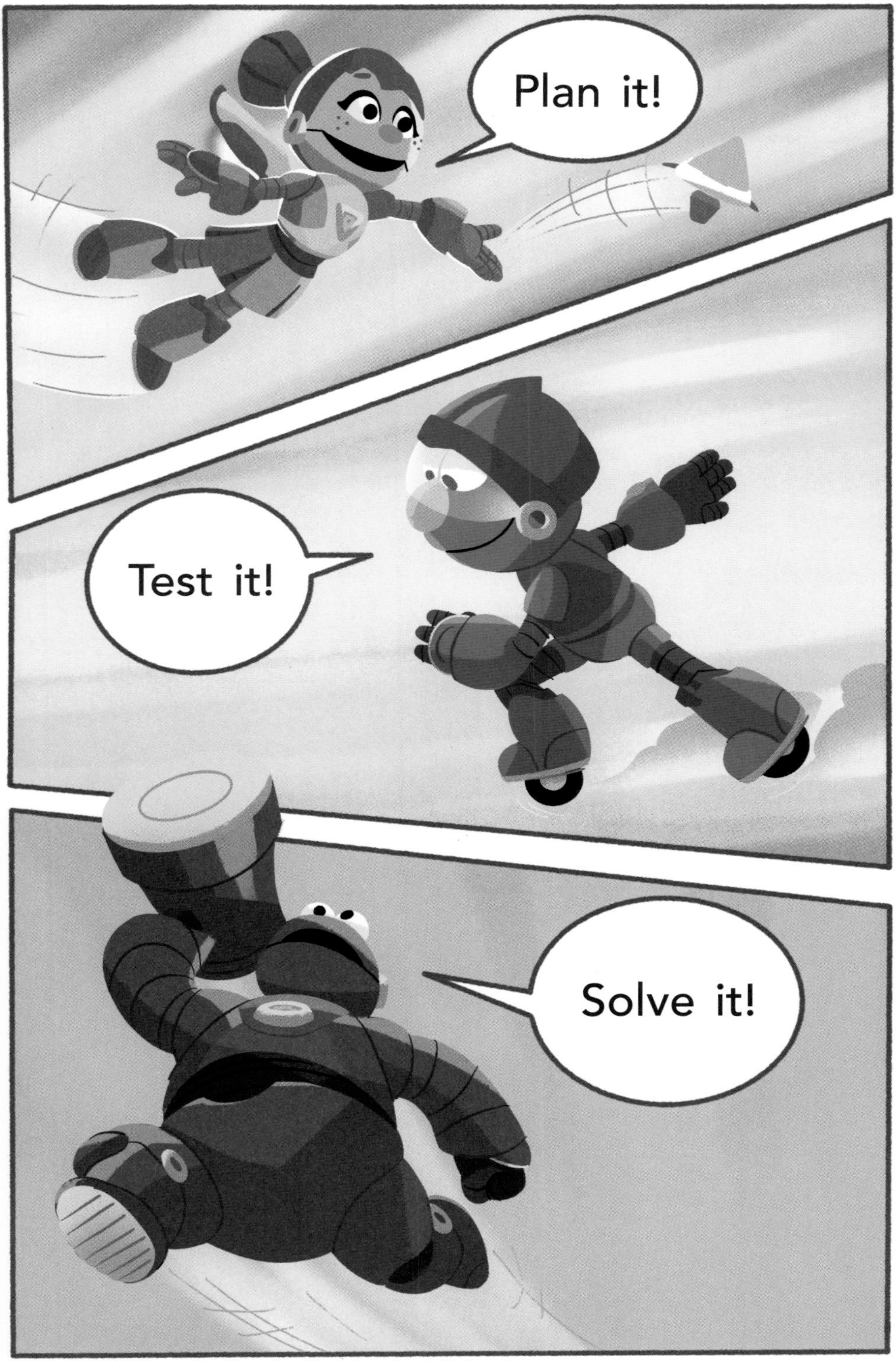
Plan it!
Test it!
Solve it!

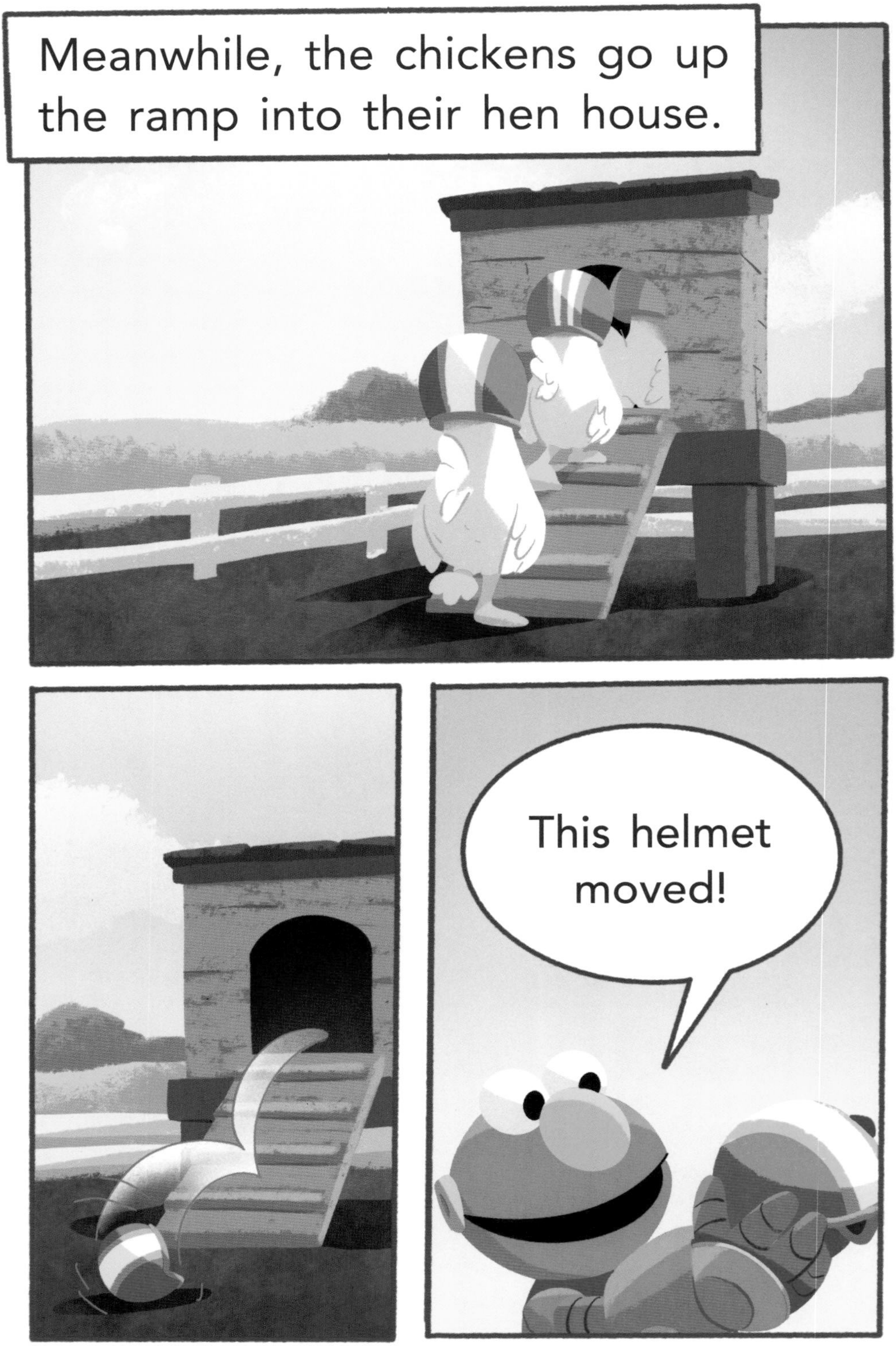
Meanwhile, the chickens go up the ramp into their hen house.
This helmet moved!

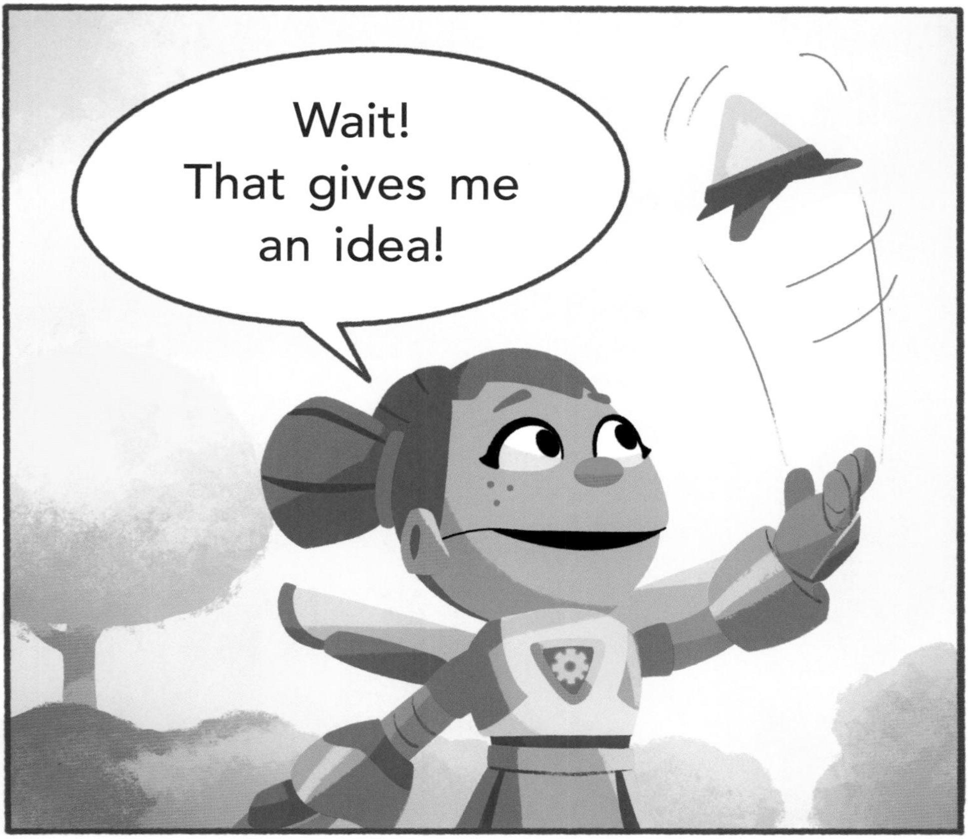
Wait!
That gives me
an idea!

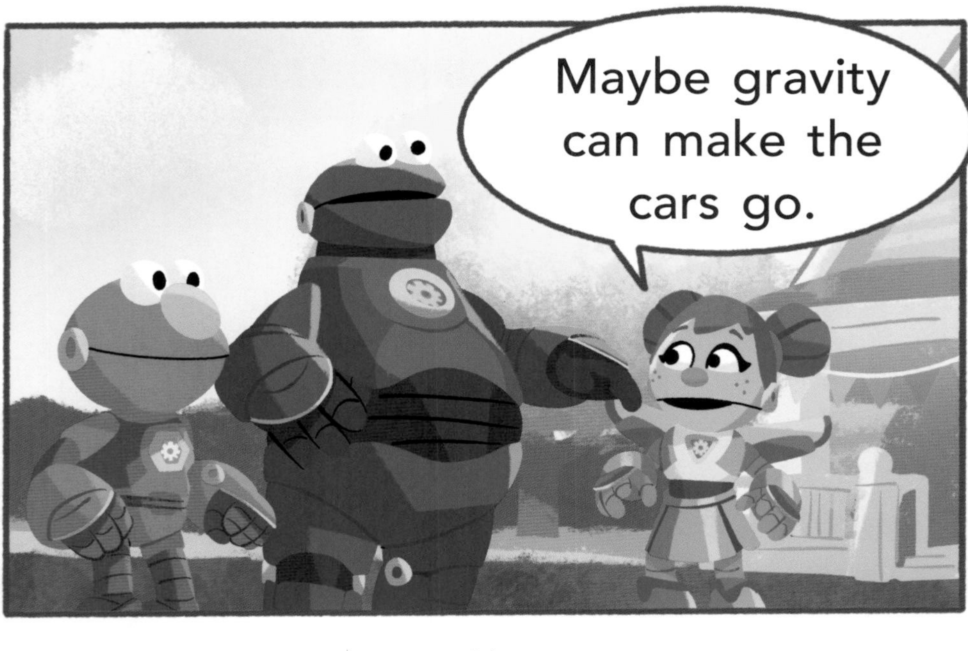
Maybe gravity
can make the
cars go.

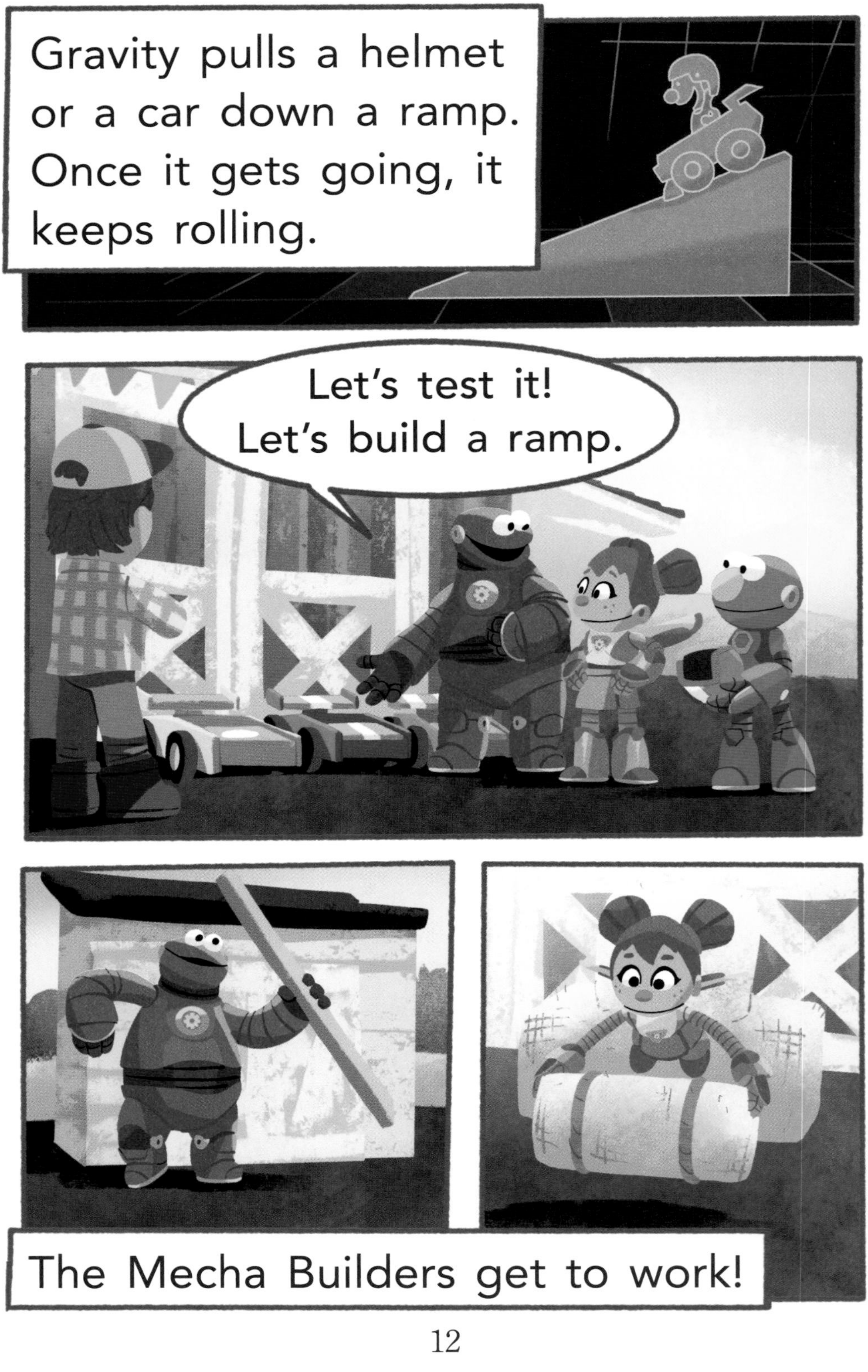
Gravity pulls a helmet or a car down a ramp. Once it gets going, it keeps rolling.
Let's test it! Let's build a ramp.
The Mecha Builders get to work!

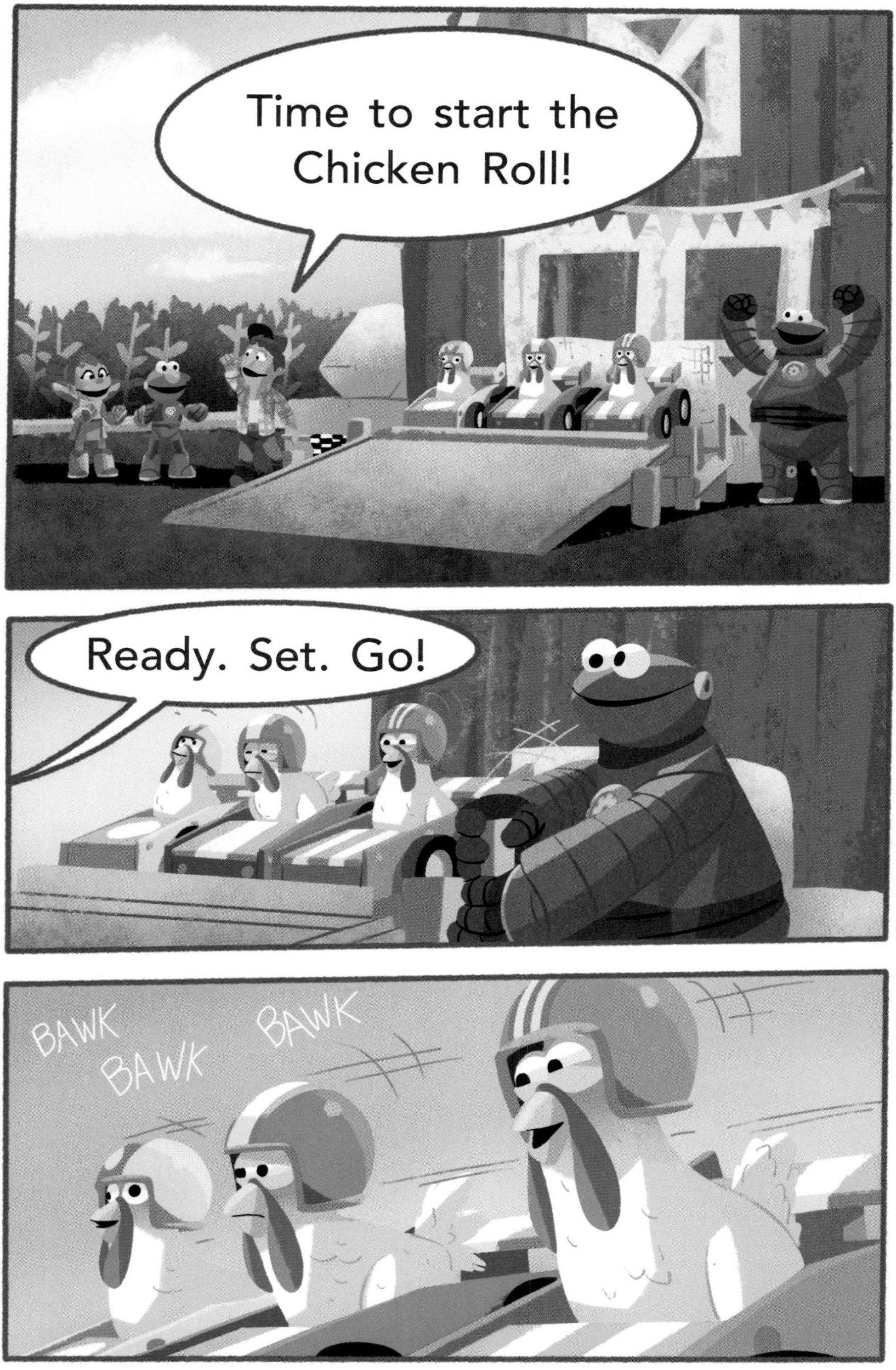
Time to start the Chicken Roll!
Ready. Set. Go!
BAWK
BAWK
BAWK

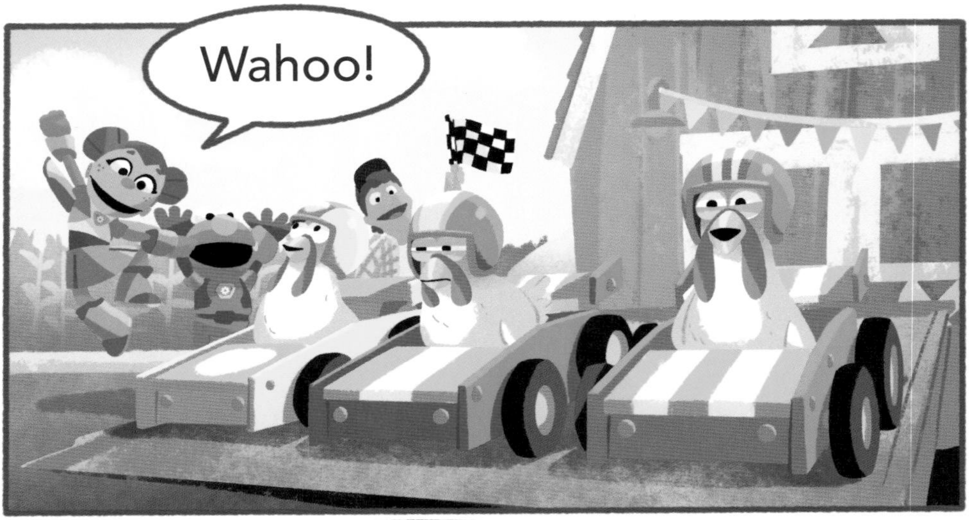
Wahoo!

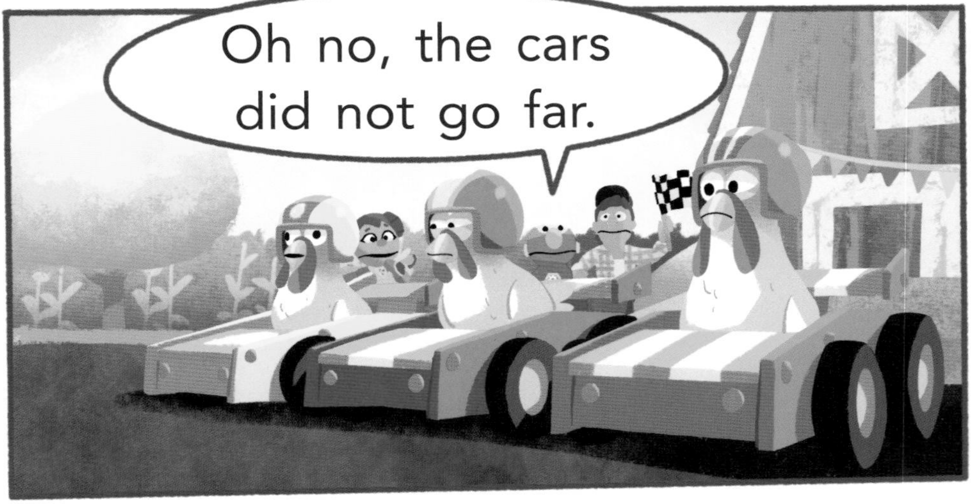
Oh no, the cars did not go far.

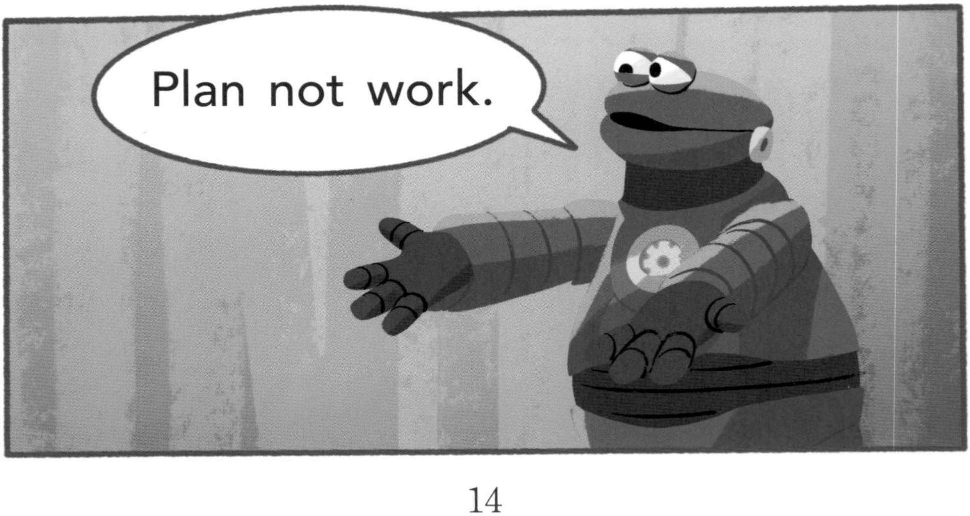
Plan not work.

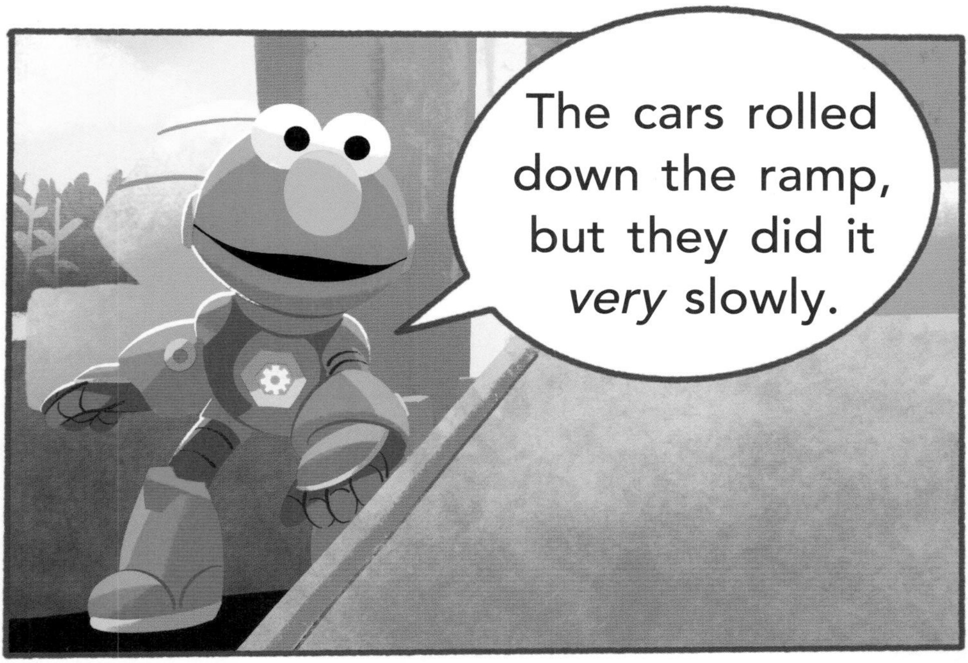
The cars rolled down the ramp, but they did it *very* slowly.

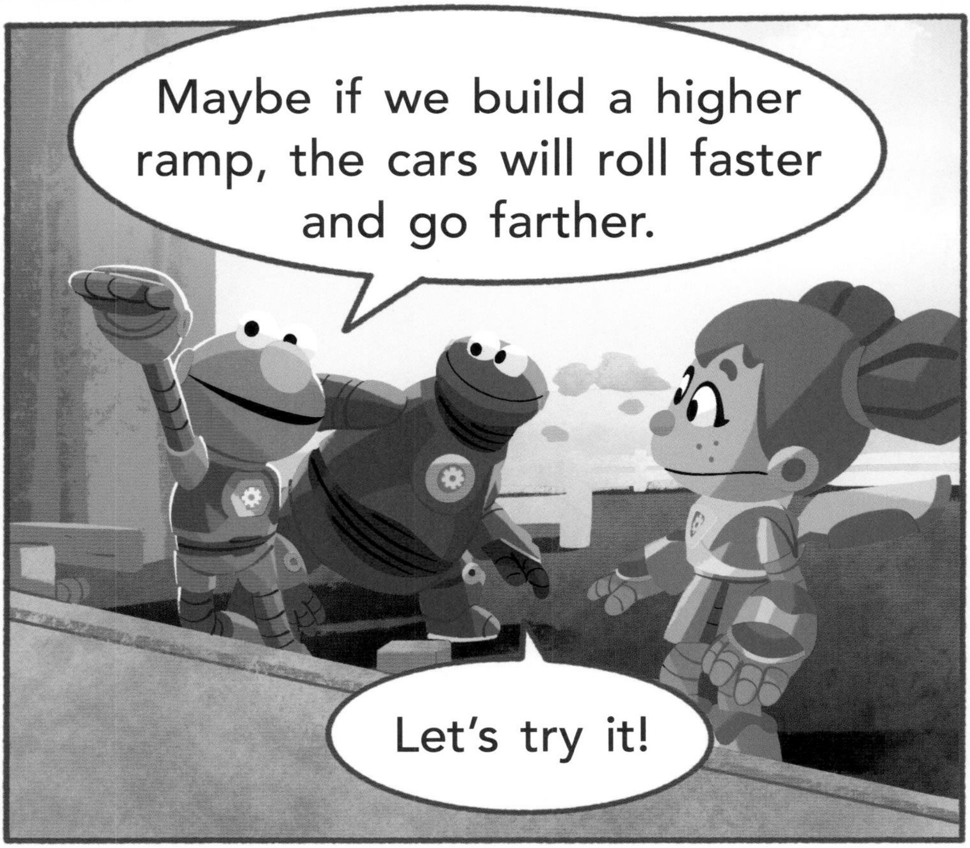
Maybe if we build a higher ramp, the cars will roll faster and go farther.
Let's try it!

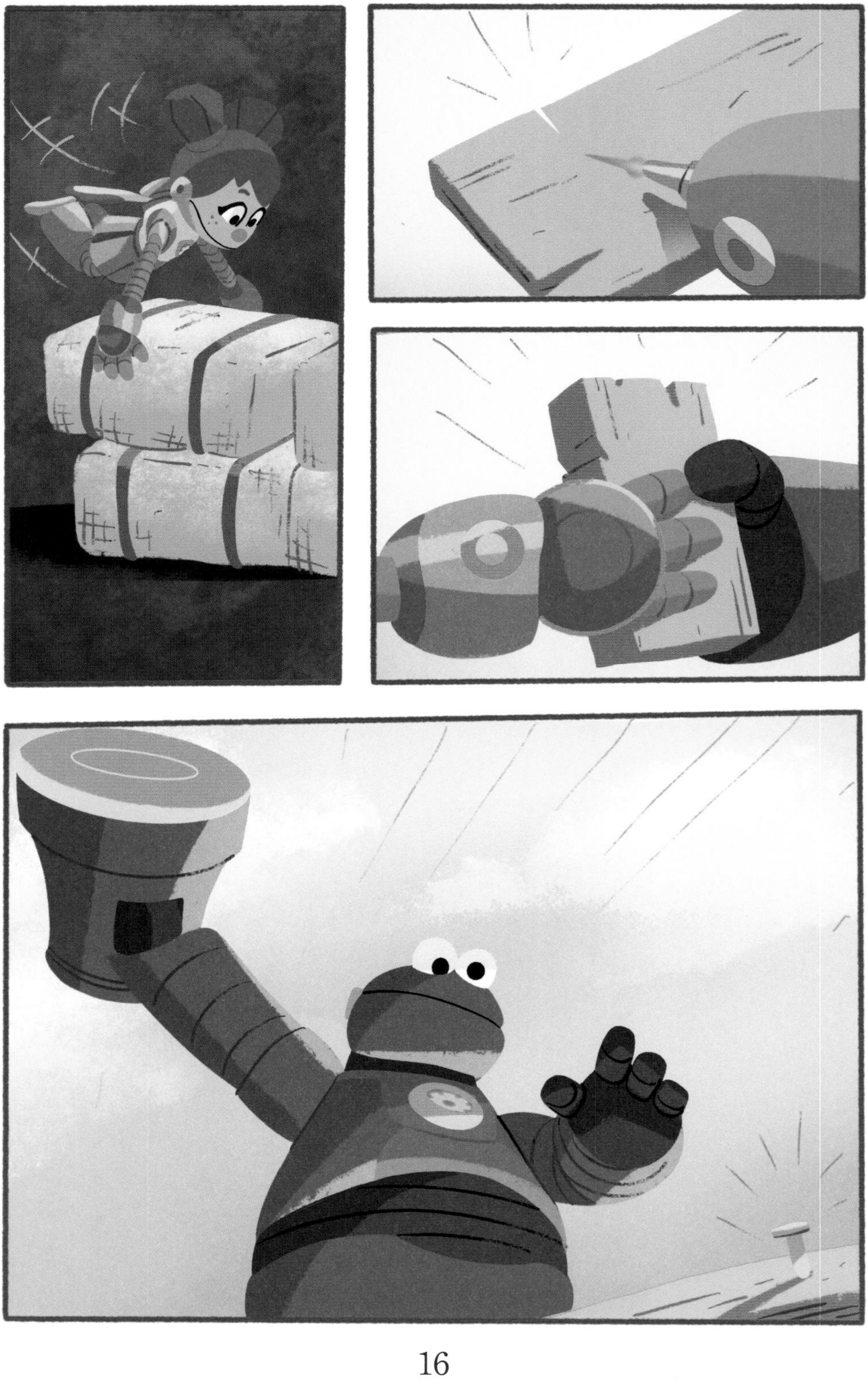

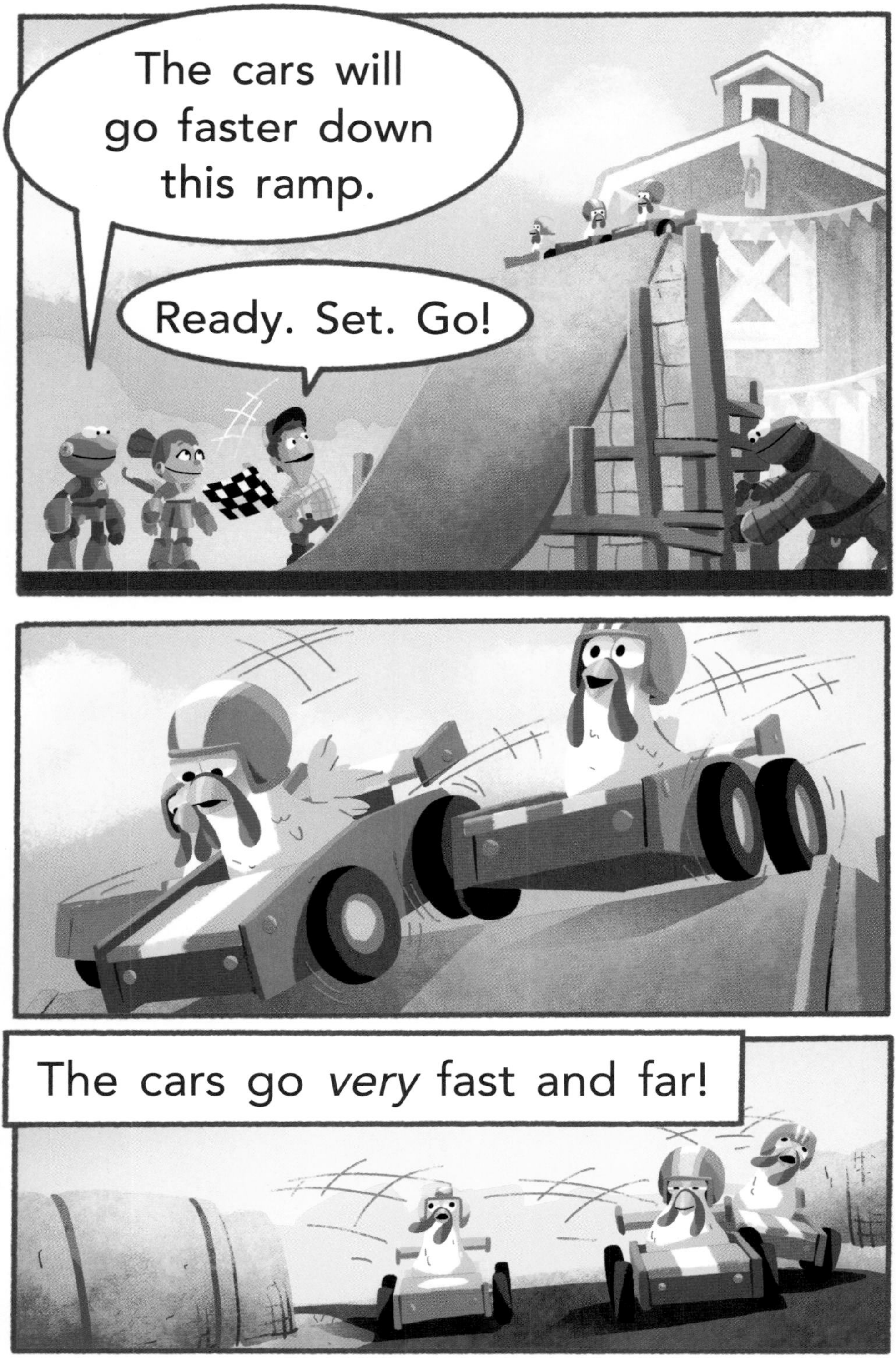
The cars will go faster down this ramp.
Ready. Set. Go!
The cars go *very* fast and far!

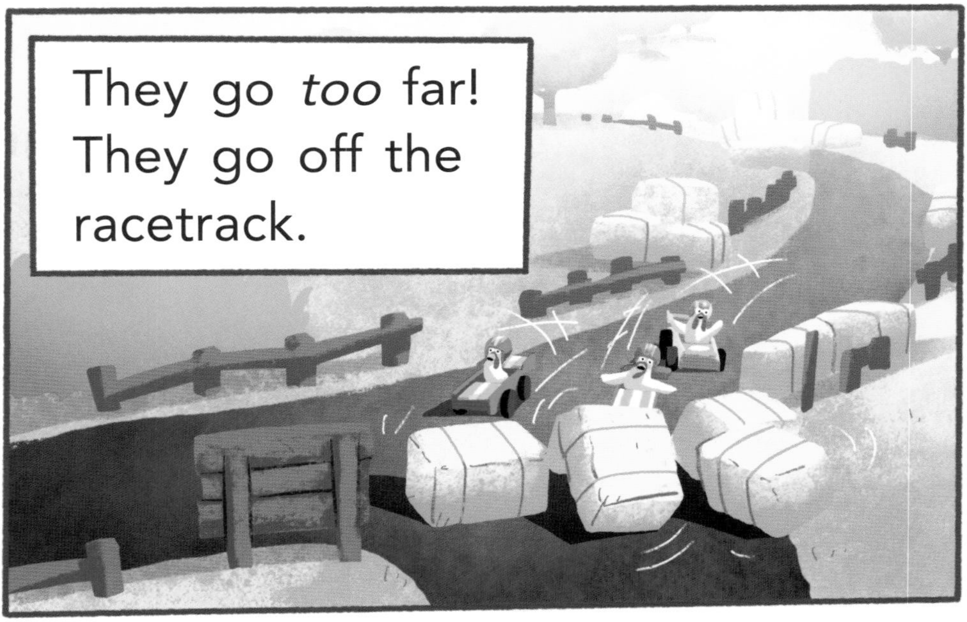
They go *too* far!
They go off the
racetrack.

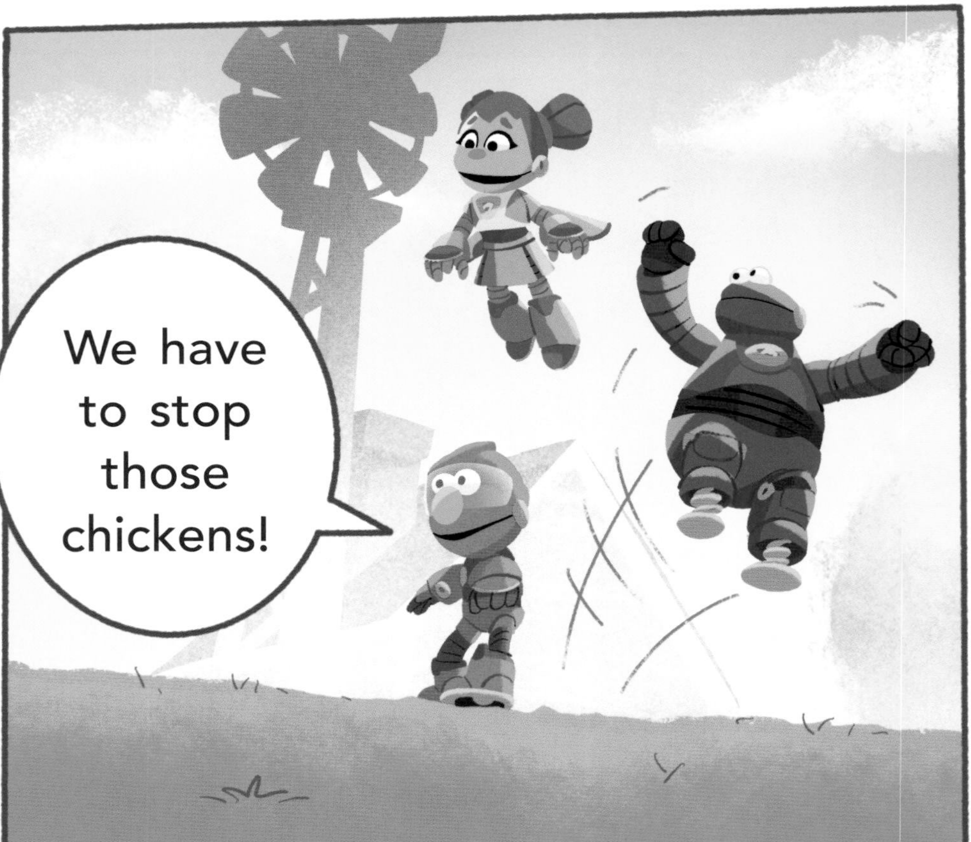
We have
to stop
those
chickens!

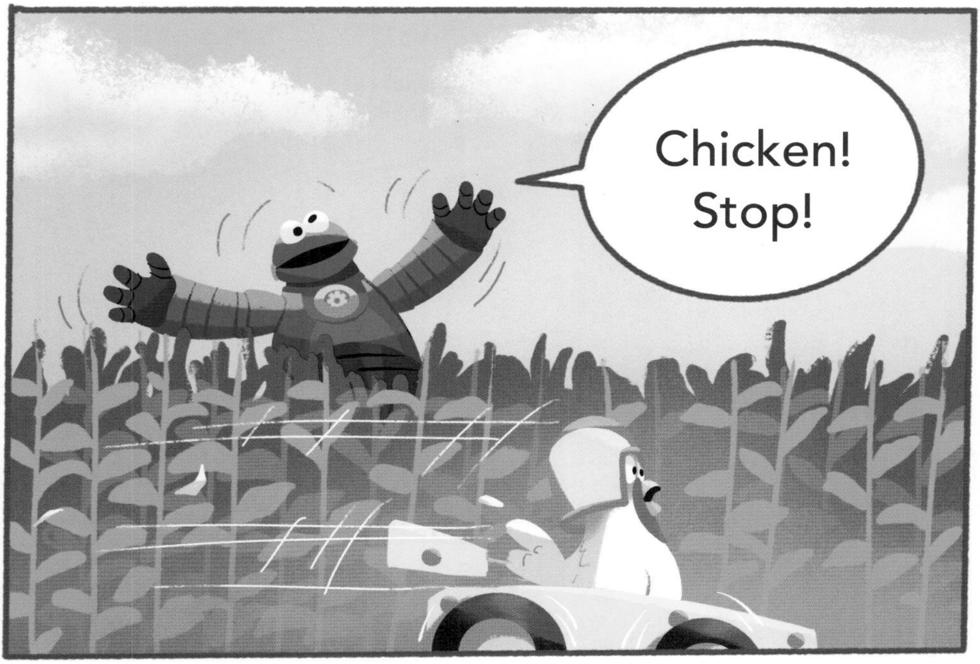
Chicken!
Stop!

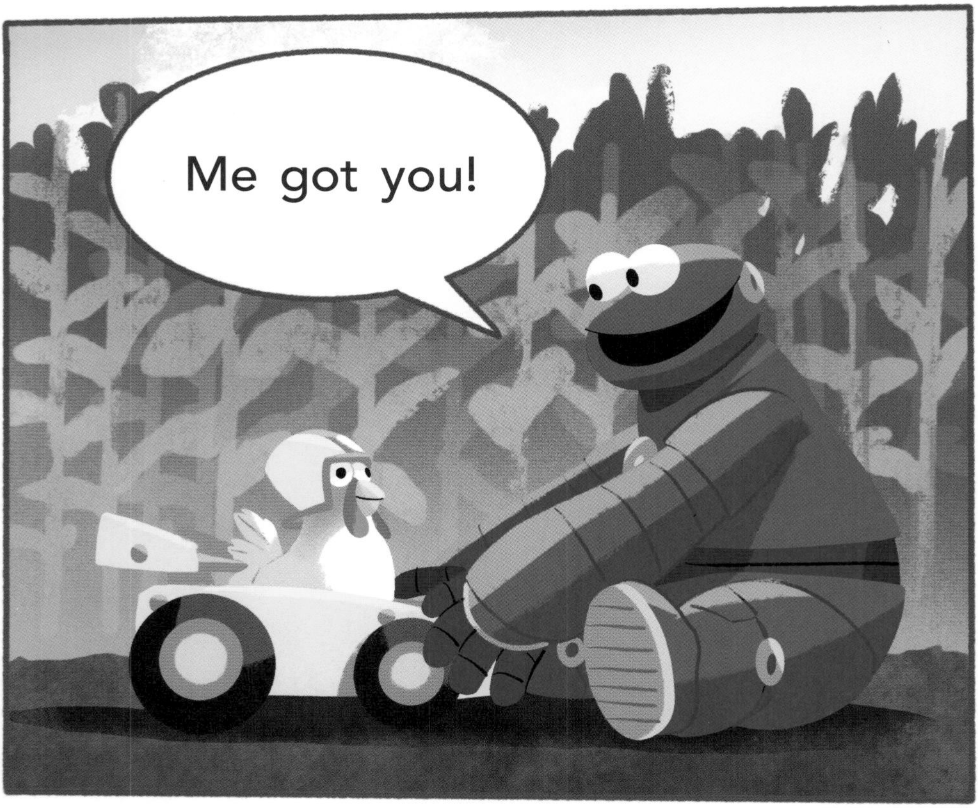
Me got you!

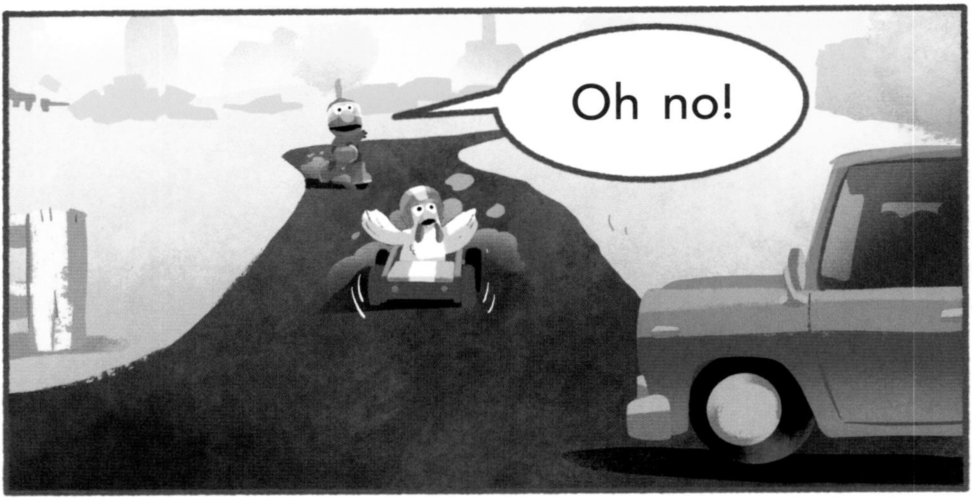
Oh no!
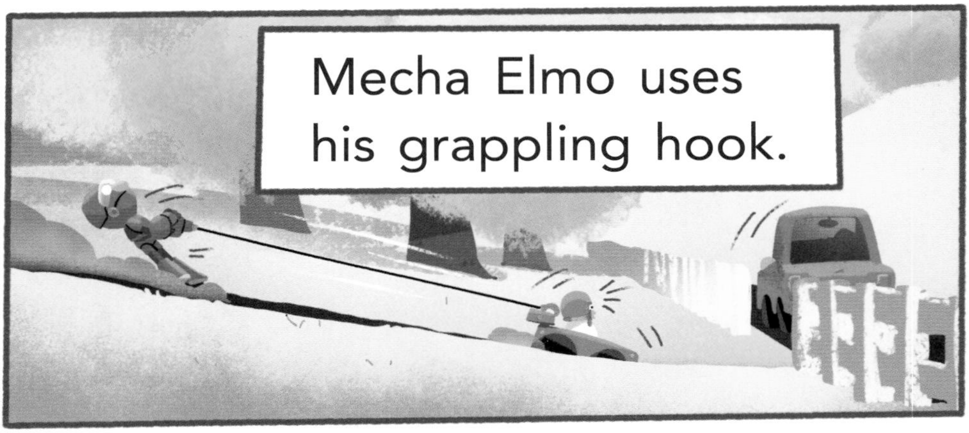
Mecha Elmo uses
his grappling hook.
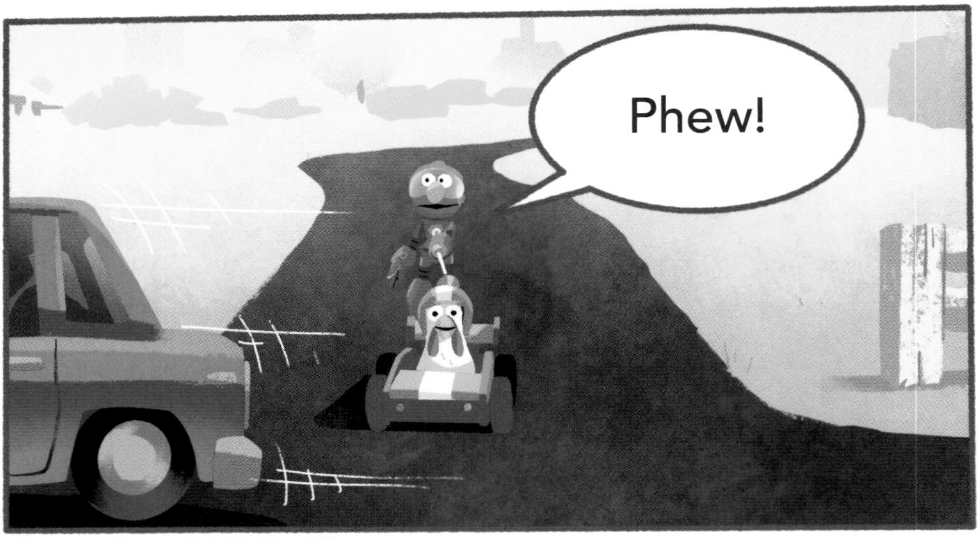
Phew!

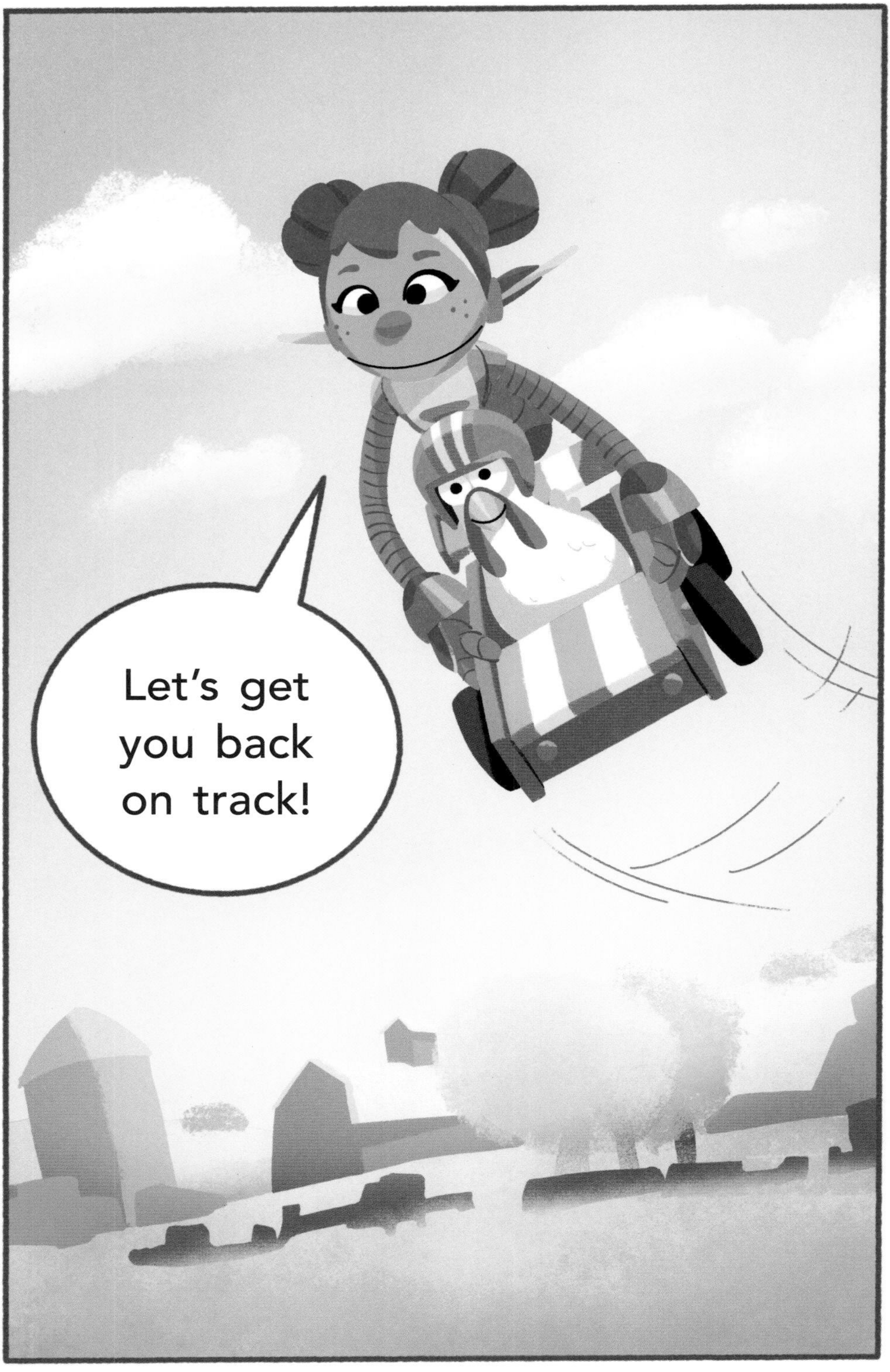
Let's get you back on track!

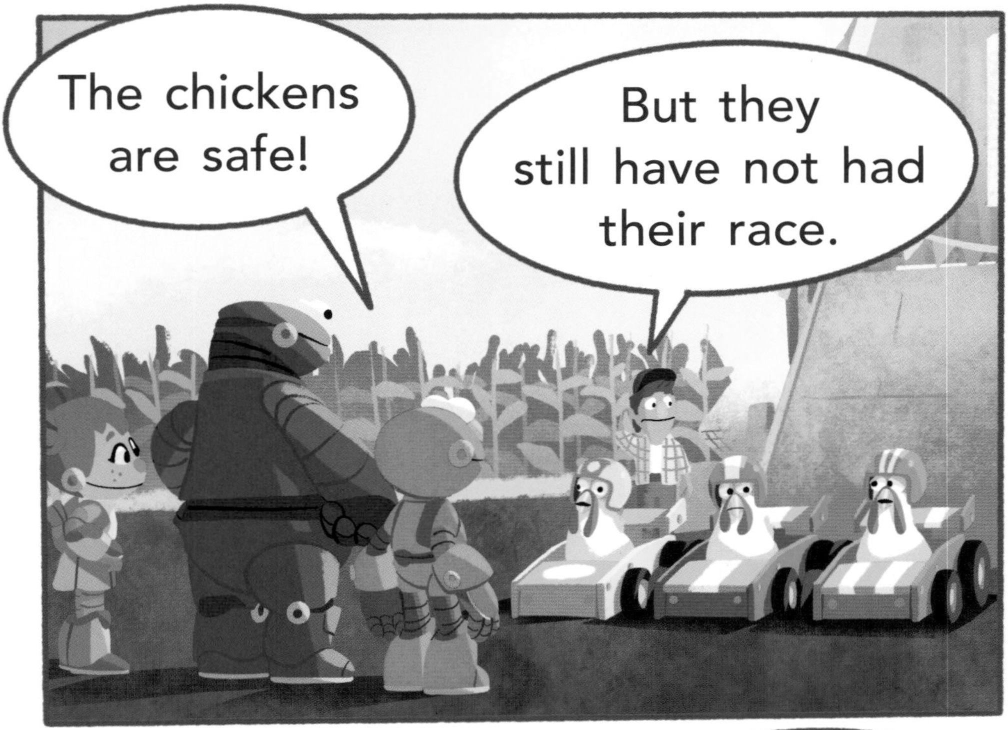
The chickens are safe!
But they still have not had their race.

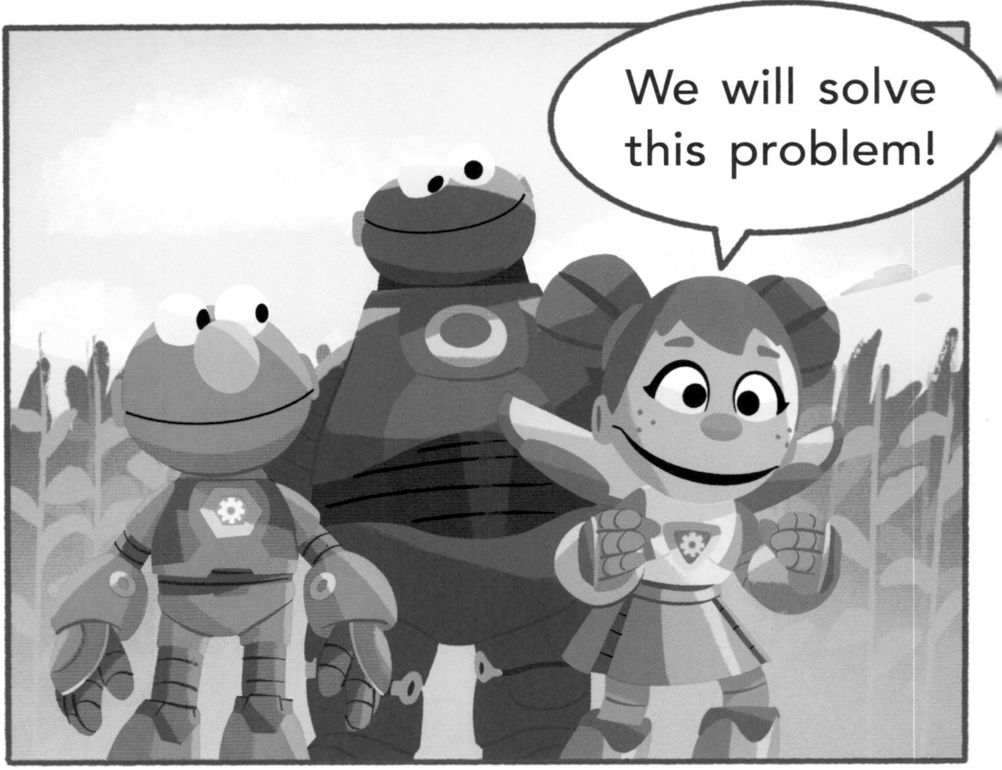
We will solve this problem!

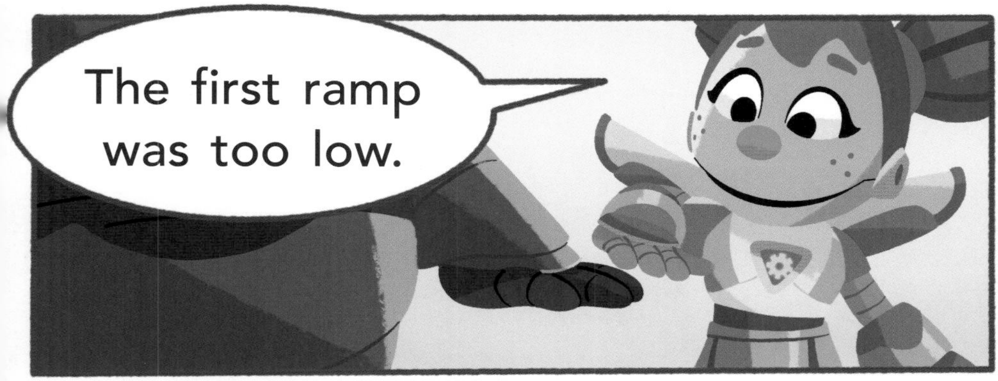
The first ramp was too low.

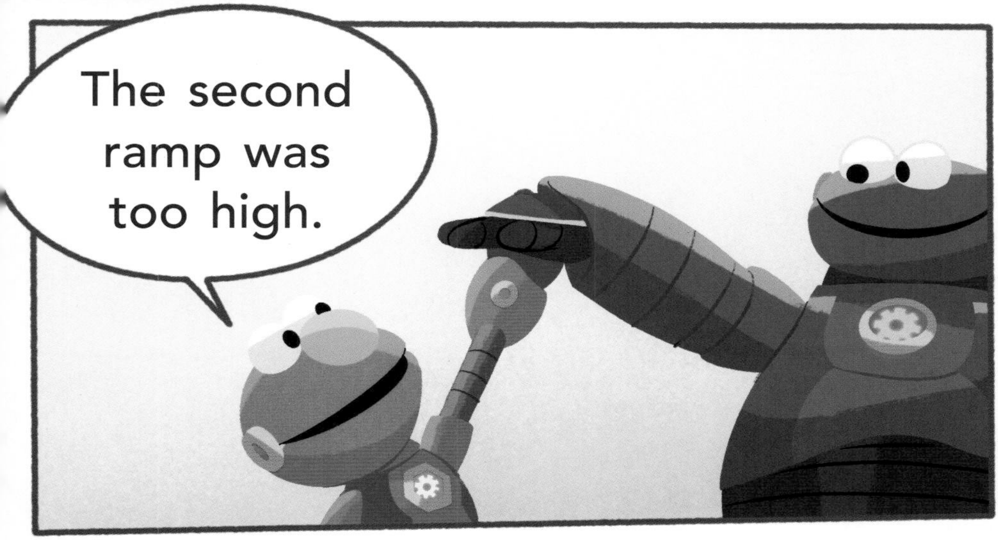
The second ramp was too high.

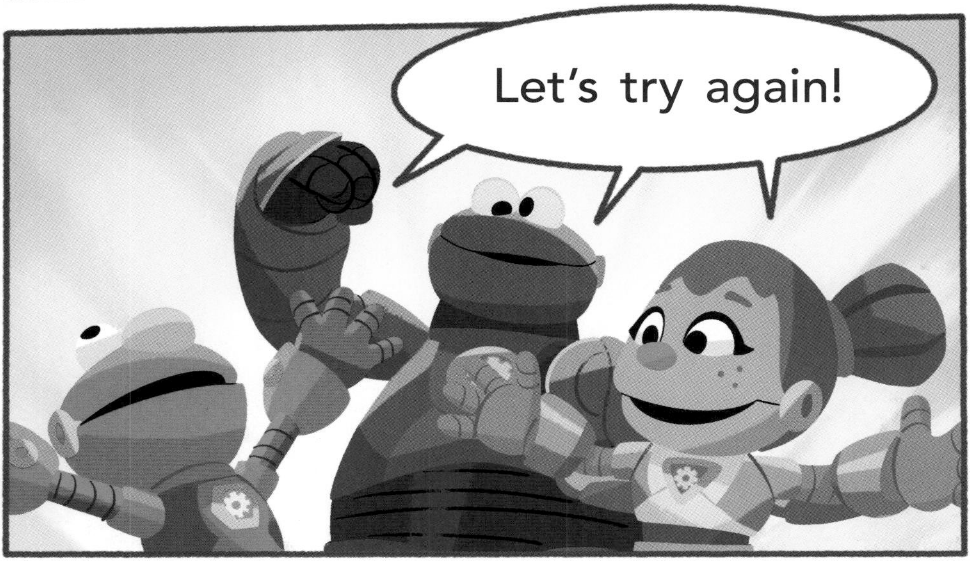
Let's try again!

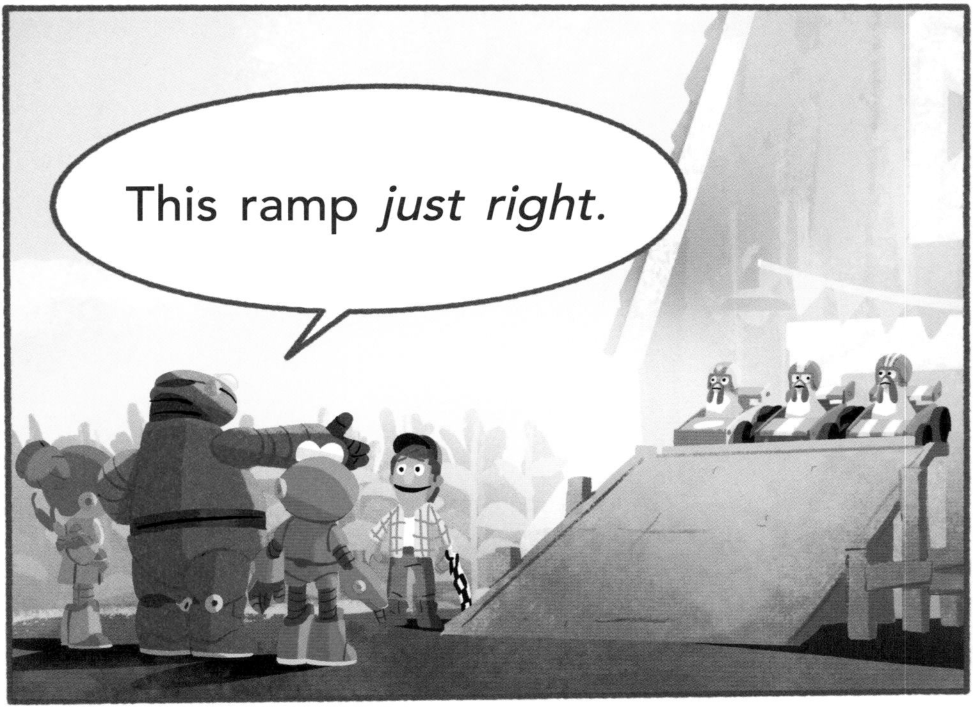
This ramp *just right.*

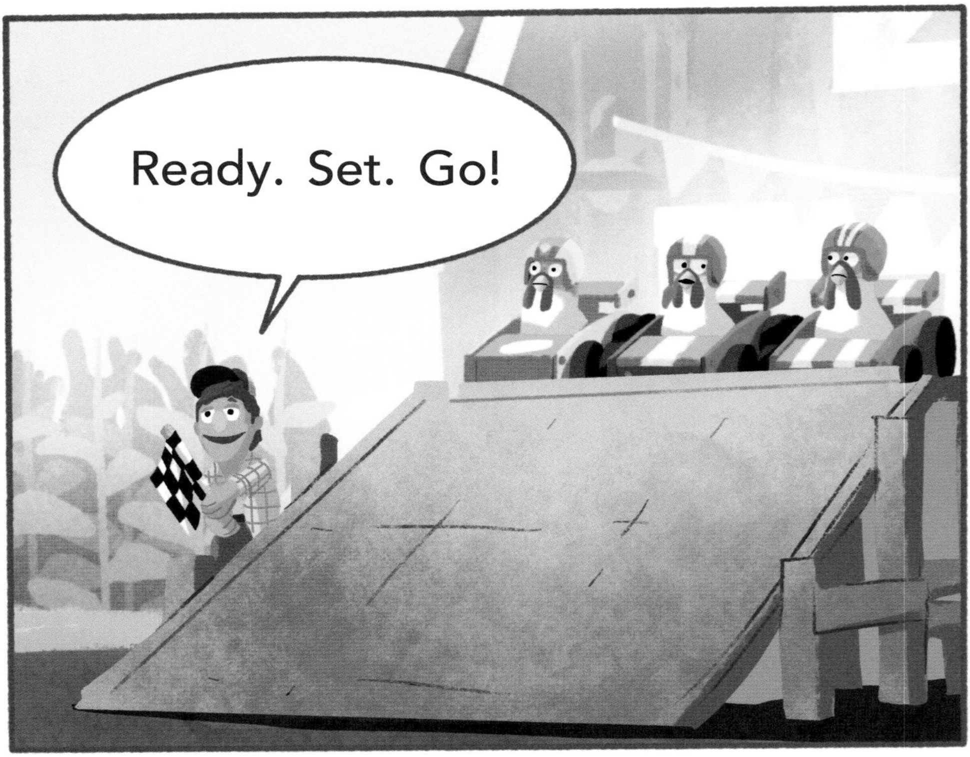
Ready. Set. Go!

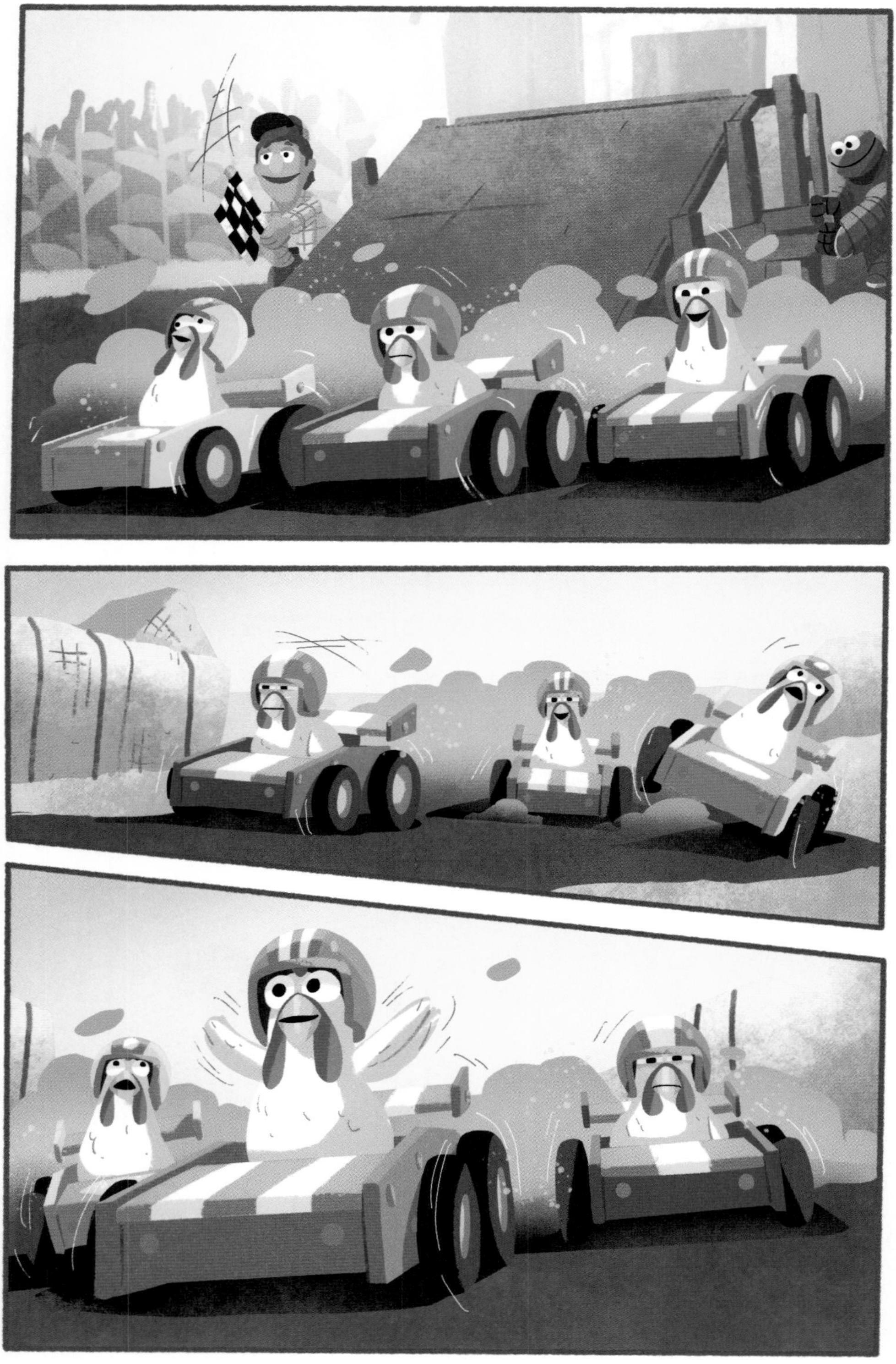

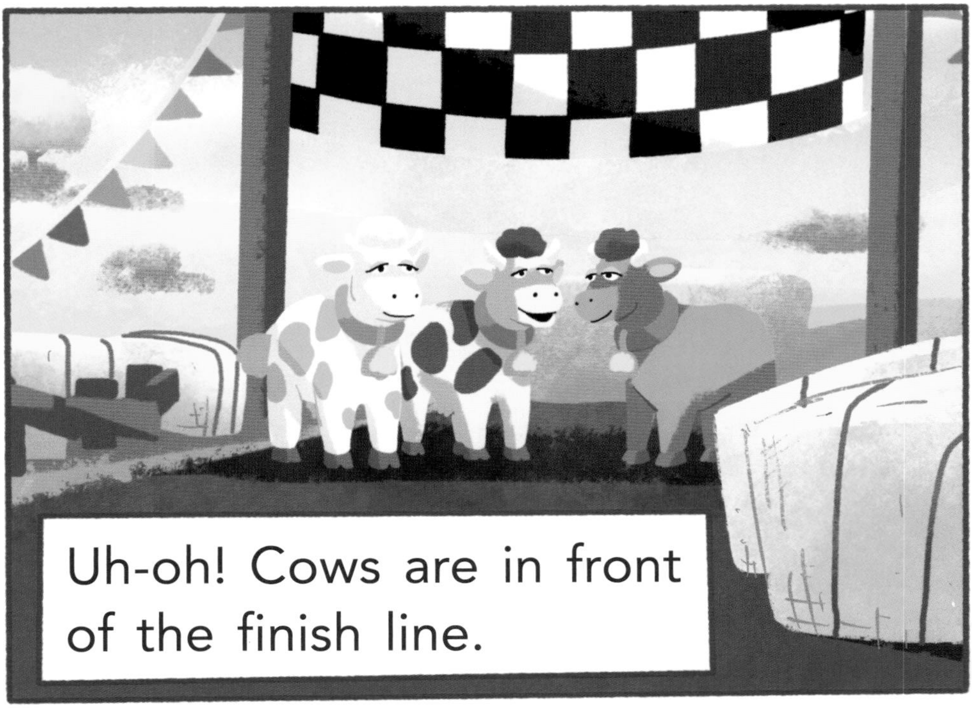
Uh-oh! Cows are in front of the finish line.

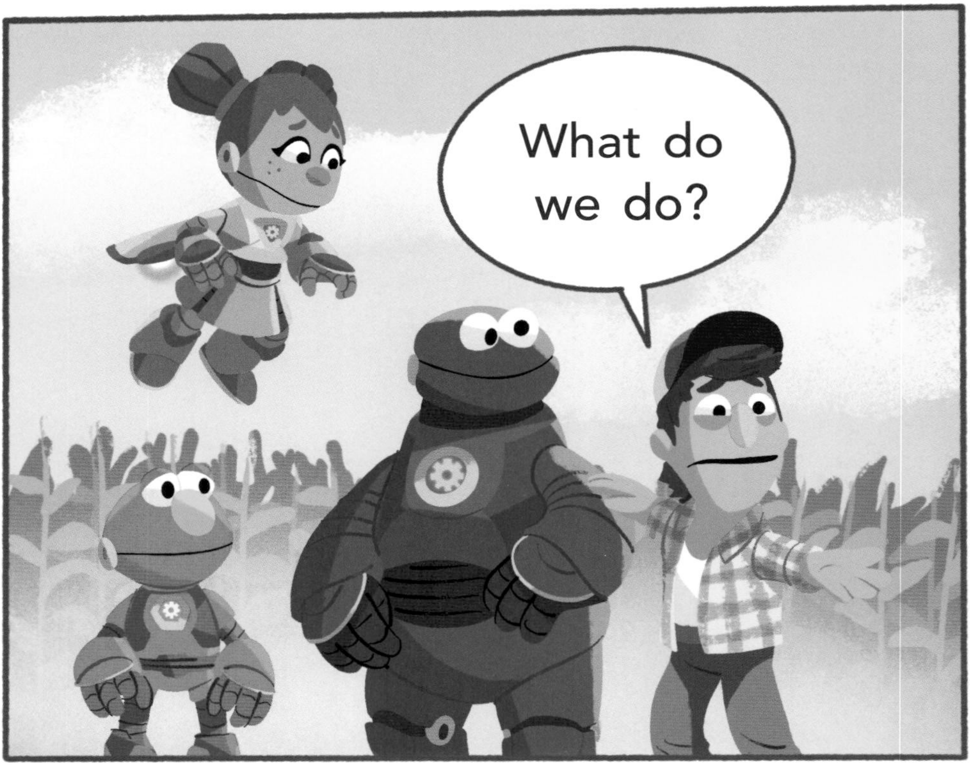
What do we do?

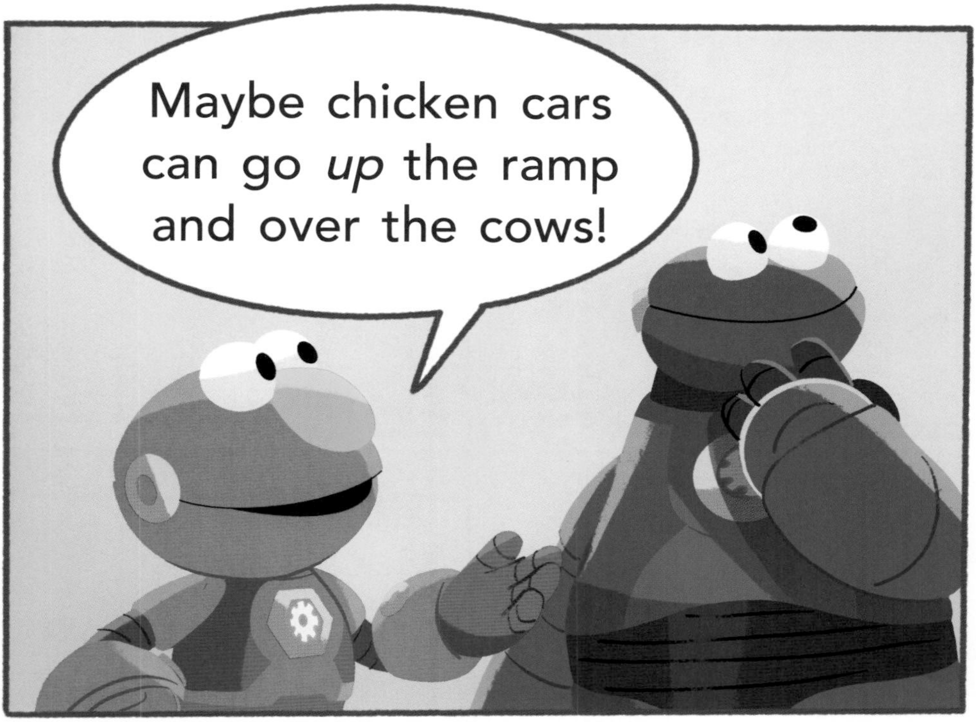
Maybe chicken cars can go *up* the ramp and over the cows!

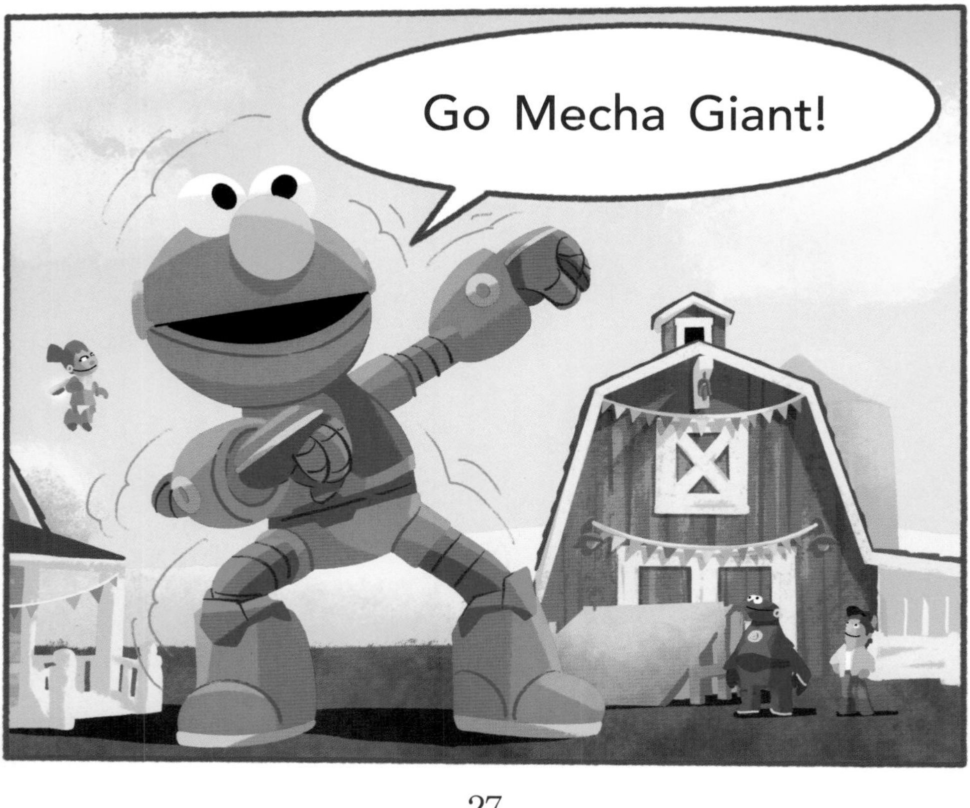
Go Mecha Giant!

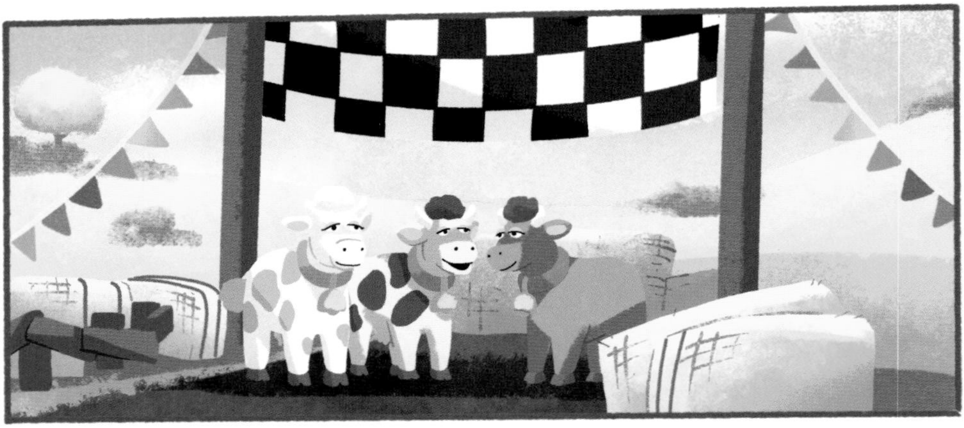

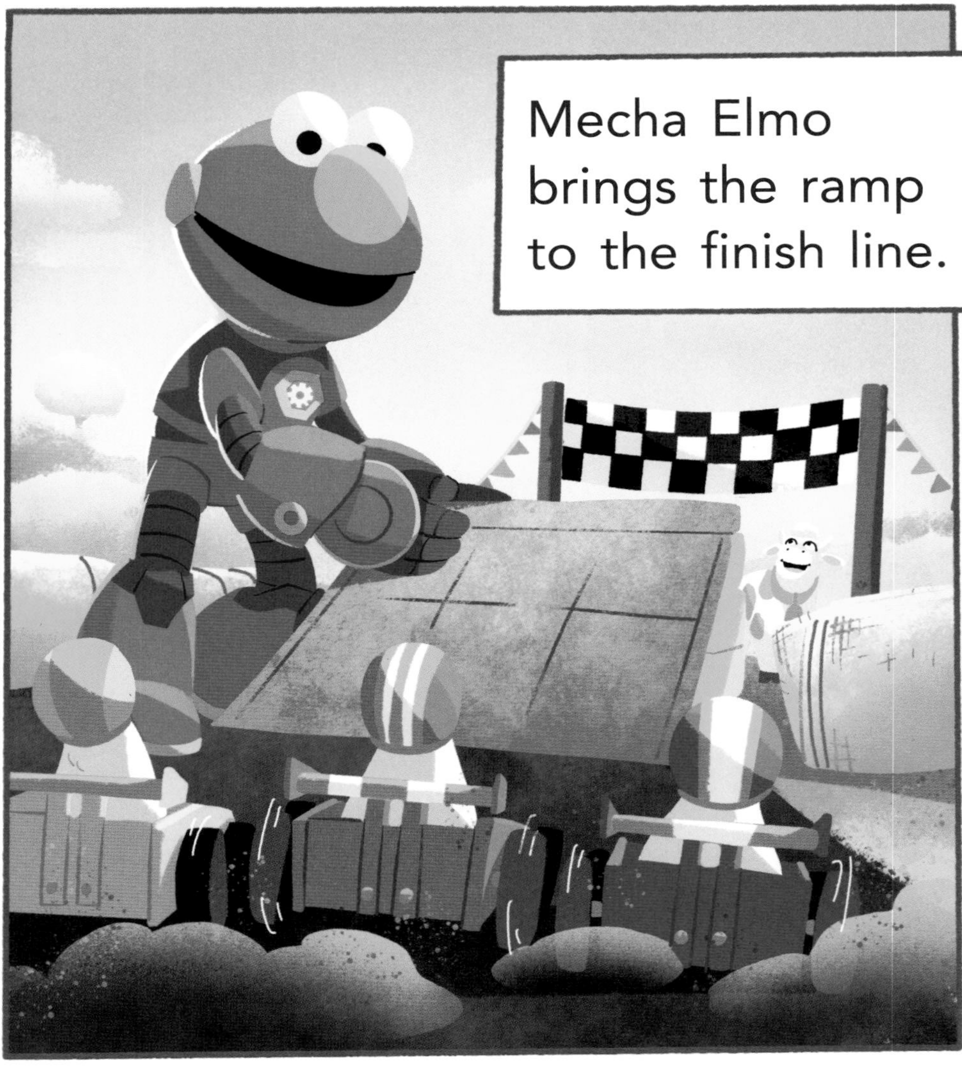
Mecha Elmo brings the ramp to the finish line.

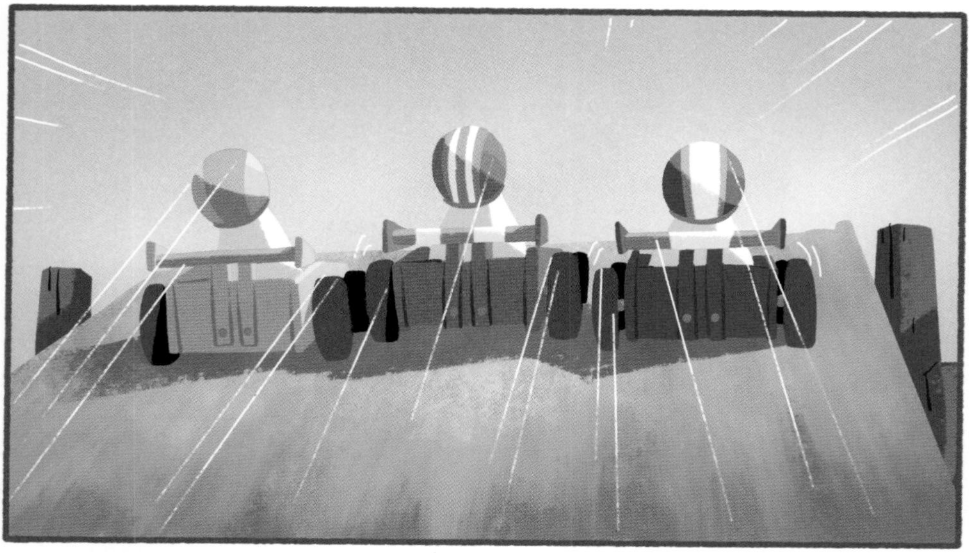

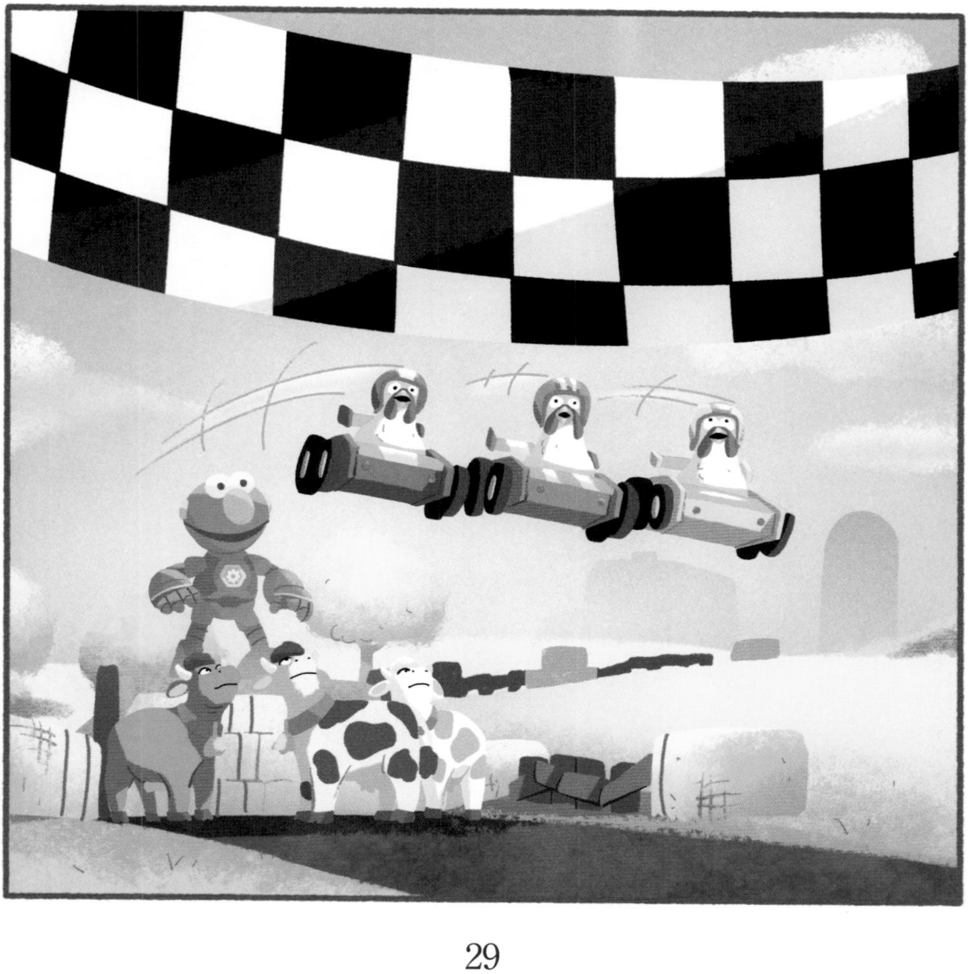

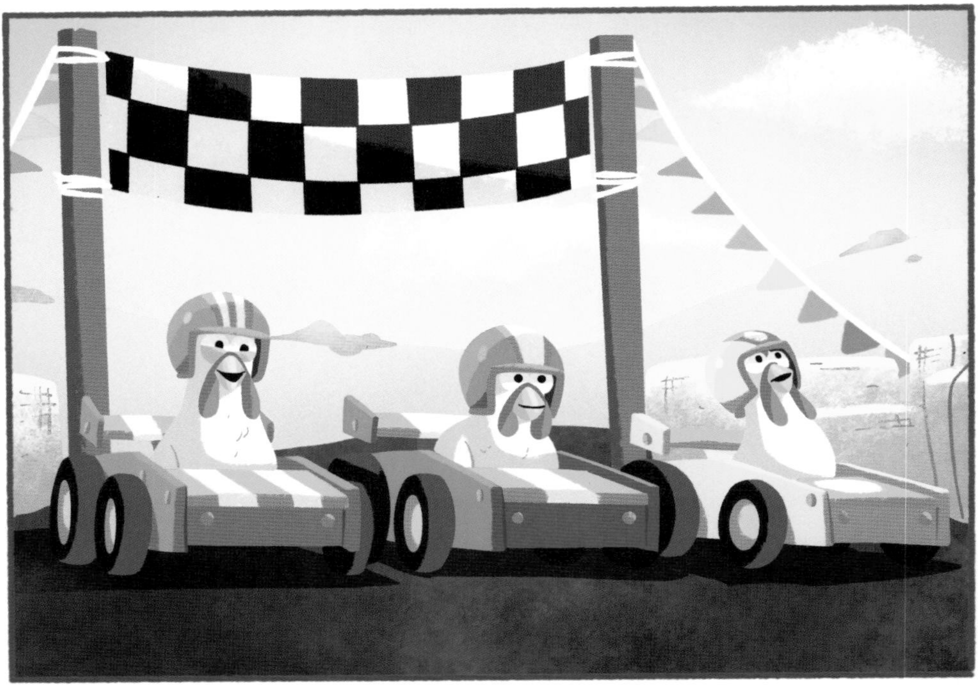

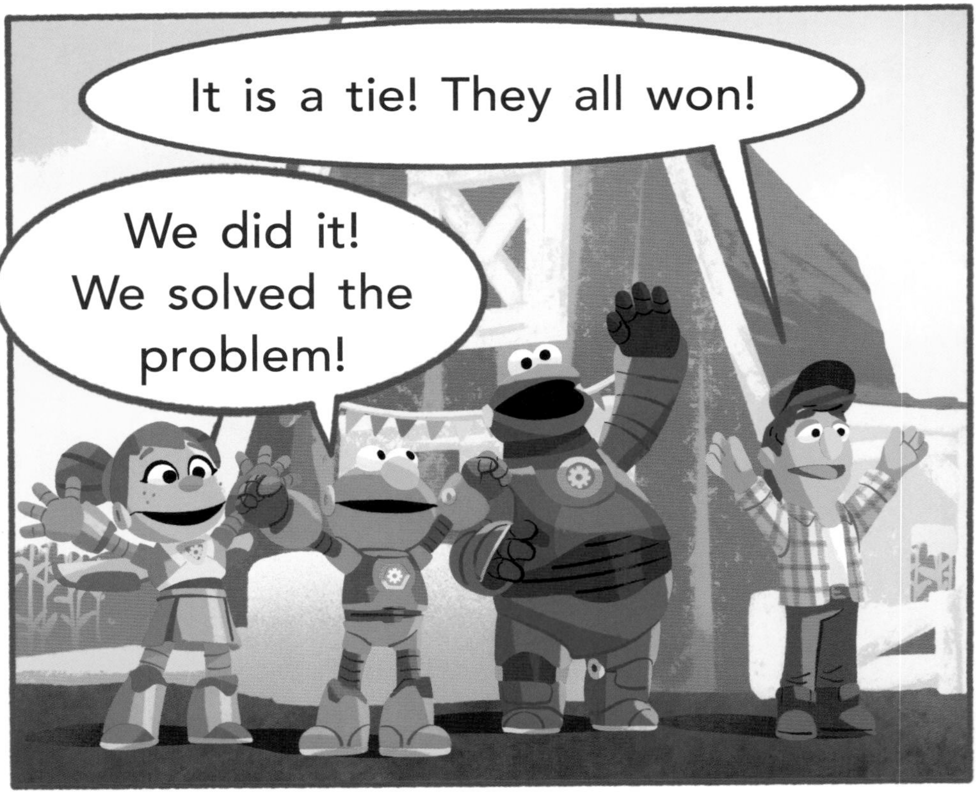
It is a tie! They all won!
We did it! We solved the problem!

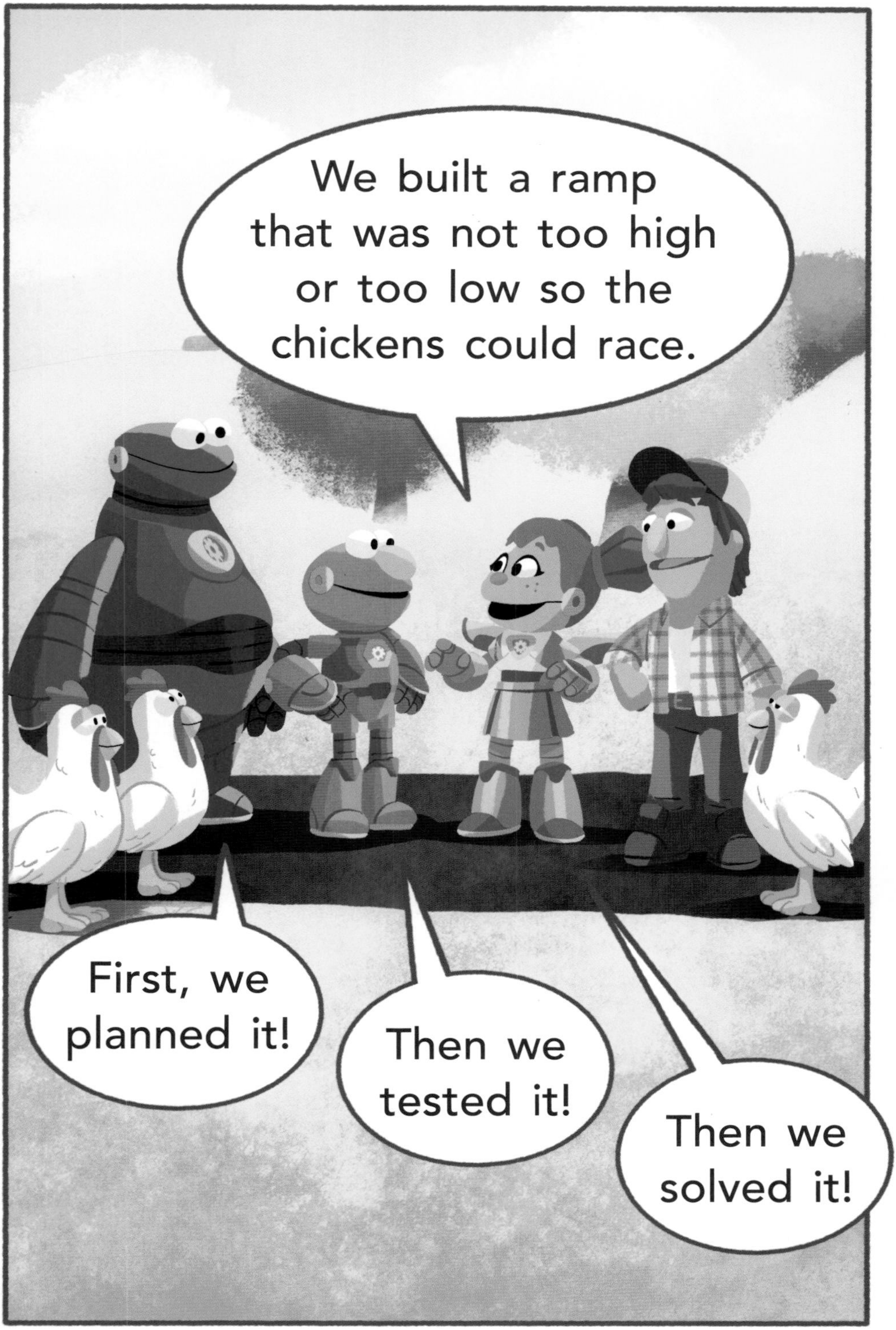
We built a ramp that was not too high or too low so the chickens could race.
First, we planned it!
Then we tested it!
Then we solved it!

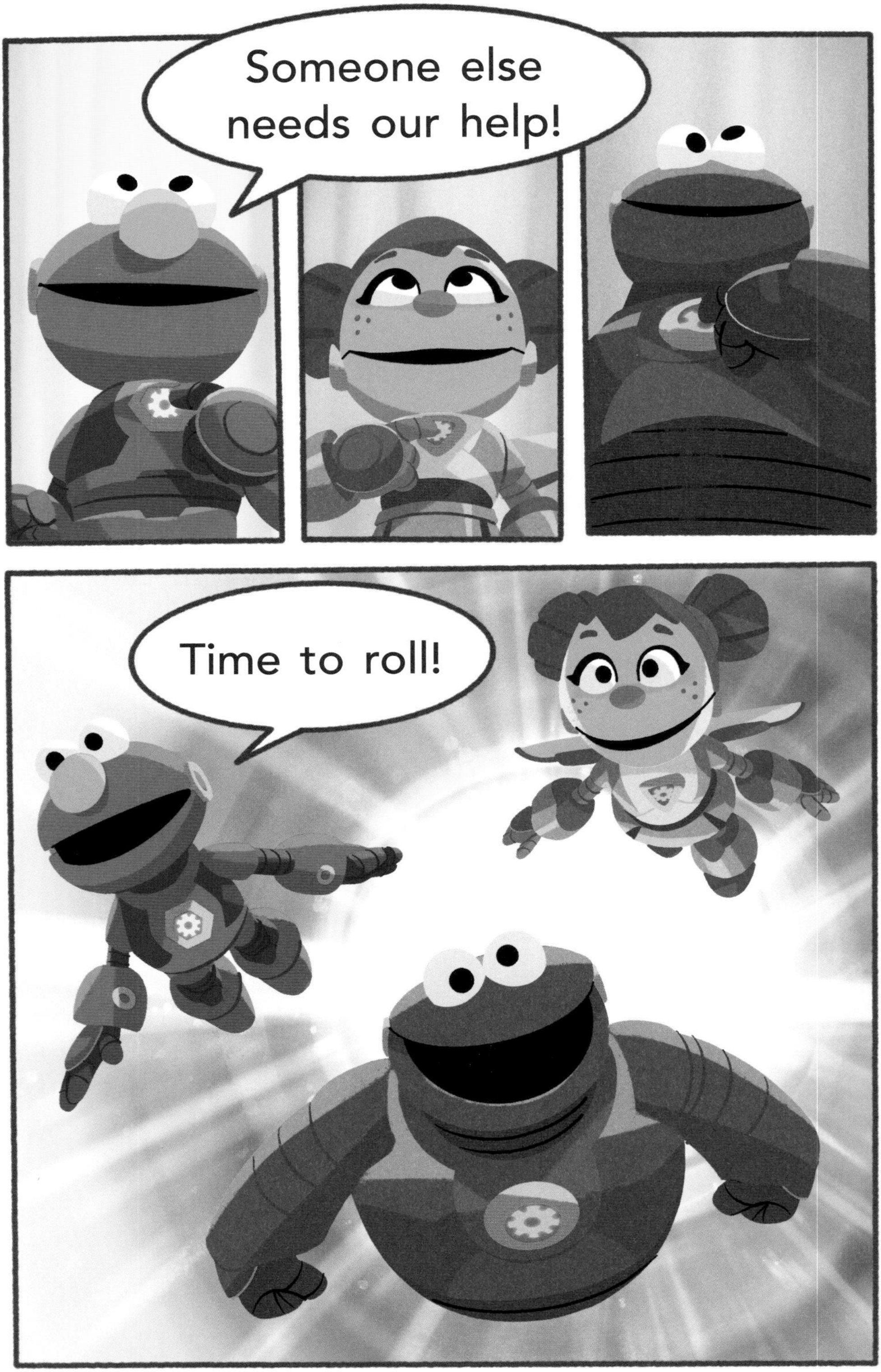
Someone else needs our help!
Time to roll!